Mac let Nikki walk ahead of him under the wooden arch and onto the Bent Tree grounds.

He nearly ran into her when she spun around, hands on her hips.

"Just tell me one thing," she whispered fiercely. "Is that what you call being comfortable with your employer?"

"What are you talking about?" he asked, confused by her sudden anger.

"All that dancing and touching and teasing."

"Nikki, Jules O'Brien and I have known each other since we were kids. She's like a sister to me."

Her eyes narrowed. "Why didn't you tell me you knew her?"

She looked so cute when she was angry, the urge to touch her was almost unbearable. Mac stuck his hands into his pockets. Was it possible she was the tiniest bit jealous?

Dear Reader,

On any given day in the U.S., there are half a million children in foster care. The goal of foster care is to provide short-term care for children who have been voluntarily or involuntarily removed from their homes, until the child can be returned to their family, adopted, or there can be a permanent transfer of guardianship. Children who are found to be unable to function well in traditional foster care are often sent to a residential treatment center or a group home. The Bent Tree Boys Ranch, the fictional setting for *The Reluctant Wrangler*, is one of these.

The Reluctant Wrangler revisits the Rocking O Ranch and brings full circle the dream of Jules Vandeveer O'Brien, the heroine in *The Rodeo Rider*, to help children who have slipped through the cracks of the judicial system. When Nikki Johannson is hired as the new housemother and riding instructor at the ranch, wrangler William (Mac) MacGregor isn't convinced she's up to the job. As time goes by, Mac learns to open his heart to the boys and to Nikki. But Nikki has a secret she isn't ready to share—one that could cost her the job and the people she's grown to love if she does.

I hope you enjoy meeting and cheering for Nikki and Mac, as well as revisiting Jules, Tanner and the other friends and neighbors in Desperation, Oklahoma.

Best wishes,

Roxann

The Reluctant Wrangler

Roxann Delaney

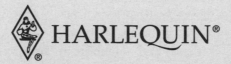

TORONTO • NEW YORK • LONDON
AMSTERDAM • PARIS • SYDNEY • HAMBURG
STOCKHOLM • ATHENS • TOKYO • MILAN • MADRID
PRAGUE • WARSAW • BUDAPEST • AUCKLAND

Recycling programs
for this product may
not exist in your area.

ISBN-13: 978-0-373-75331-4

THE RELUCTANT WRANGLER

Copyright © 2010 by Roxann Farmer

This edition published by arrangement with Harlequin Books S.A.

For questions and comments about the quality of this book please contact us at Customer_eCare@Harlequin.ca

® and TM are trademarks of the publisher. Trademarks indicated with ® are registered in the United States Patent and Trademark Office, the Canadian Trade Marks Office and in other countries.

www.eHarlequin.com

Printed in U.S.A.

ABOUT THE AUTHOR

Roxann Delaney doesn't remember a time when she wasn't reading or writing, and she always loved that touch of romance in both. A native Kansan, she's lived on a farm, in a small town, and has returned to live in the city where she was born. Her four daughters and grandchildren keep her busy when she isn't writing or designing Web sites. The 1999 Maggie Award winner is excited to be a part of Harlequin American Romance and loves to hear from readers. Contact her at roxann@roxanndelaney.com or visit her Web site, www.roxanndelaney.com.

Books by Roxann Delaney

HARLEQUIN AMERICAN ROMANCE
1194—FAMILY BY DESIGN
1269—THE RODEO RIDER
1292—BACHELOR COWBOY
1313—THE LAWMAN'S LITTLE SURPRISE

Don't miss any of our special offers. Write to us at the following address for information on our newest releases.

Harlequin Reader Service
U.S.: 3010 Walden Ave., P.O. Box 1325, Buffalo, NY 14269
Canadian: P.O. Box 609, Fort Erie, Ont. L2A 5X3

Love and kisses to my newest granddaughter, Payton McKenzy, our miracle baby, who spent her first two months struggling for life after open heart surgery, and is home healthy, happy and growing.

Chapter One

"Welcome to the Bent Tree."

Nikki Johannson took the outstretched hand of the woman who was now her employer and hoped Jules O'Brien didn't notice how nervous she was. She hadn't expected to get the job as housemother for a group of boys ranging in age from eight to fifteen years old, but the moment she'd read the newspaper article about the Bent Tree Boys Ranch, she knew she had to try. Had it been only a week since she'd been hired?

"Thank you for the opportunity to work here, Mrs. O'Brien," Nikki said, releasing her hand.

"Please, call me Jules. We're all family here, and no one calls me Mrs. O'Brien."

Nikki tried for her best smile, struck by the word *family* and how close it was to the secret she kept. "I'm sure I'll enjoy working here, Jules."

Lines formed between Jules's eyes. "You're certain you want to take on giving the boys riding lessons, too?" she asked. "I don't want to burden you with extra duties, and I'm sure we can find someone else if—"

"I don't mind at all," Nikki replied. "I'm looking forward to it."

The frown on her new employer's face disappeared, replaced by a grateful smile. "You have the experience to do it, but if it should get to be too much for you, we'll make other arrangements."

Before Nikki had a chance to answer, a tall man approached them, looking too polished for an Oklahoma ranch.

"You needed to ask me something?" he asked when he stopped near Jules. His voice was deep and smooth as he glanced at Nikki.

Nikki noticed a glint of arrogance in his baby-blue eyes as he returned his attention to Jules. His aquiline nose and chiseled square jaw would make any woman take a second look. Nikki swallowed hard. She knew enough about the O'Briens to know the man wasn't Jules's husband, and she wondered who he was.

"Thank you for coming so quickly, Mac," Jules greeted him, then turned to Nikki. "This is William MacGregor, better known as Mac, our head wrangler at Bent Tree. Our only wrangler at the moment," she added, turning to smile at him. "Mac, Nikki Johannson is our new housemother."

"Nice to meet you," he said without looking directly at her.

Nikki was surprised to learn he was a ranch hand. He looked nothing like the few she'd met, and he certainly wasn't anything like the cowboys she'd known.

Jules turned to the man again. "Since you're in charge of the horses for the boys, Mac, you should know that she'll also be teaching the boys to ride."

He slid a look at Nikki that made her skin prickle. "We don't have a lot of horses at present, but we'll be getting in more stock."

"We'll be adding a few more boys soon, too," Jules said thoughtfully, and turned to Nikki. "You do know that these boys have had serious problems in their lives.

A few have been in trouble with the law, although none of them are dangerous."

Nikki nodded. "As I mentioned, psychology is my college major, although I'm still working on my degree." Or would be, if she hadn't been forced to quit because of finances. Even with a scholarship and financial aid, she still had to work for a living, and that took up most of her time. "I've worked with boys who had similar problems at Cherokee Nation Youth Services, so I understand they need a strong, yet caring person to guide them. I assure you, I'm up to the job in that respect."

"Where was that?" Mac asked.

"In Tahlequah," Nikki answered. "I was employed at what's now known as Sequoyah Schools for four years after graduating from there, as well as having worked at a riding camp near Broken Arrow and with Youth Services."

"You're Cherokee?"

"Half Cherokee."

"That explains the Scandinavian surname."

Jules looked at her with eyes full of interest. "My husband is half Cherokee, with an Irish surname."

"Is he?" Nikki asked, as if she hadn't known. The name Johannson was on her birth certificate and her legal name, but she knew it wasn't her father's name or her mother's. Even so, there was no reason to tell either of them that.

Turning to Mac, although she yearned to know more about Jules's husband, she asked, "Have you studied the Cherokee?"

"No, I haven't." His mouth twisted into a slight smile. "But I did read *Where the Red Fern Grows* when I was a boy."

Nikki did her best to take the edge off her answer. "Not quite the same."

"I'll give you a tour of the ranch and the staff accommodations." Jules motioned for Nikki to follow her and turned to call over her shoulder. "Mac, could you meet me at the main building in about ten minutes?" His answer was a nod before he disappeared into a row of trees.

"It's very nice here," Nikki said as Jules led her under a large carved wooden sign proclaiming they were entering the Bent Tree Boys Ranch.

"I explained last week that there are two ranches on the property here," Jules continued. "The Rocking O Ranch was my husband's home before we were married. He grew up here. As a wedding gift, he gave me forty acres of what was pasture, for the purpose of building a boys' ranch. It's been a dream of mine since I was a young girl to provide a place where children—especially boys—who haven't fit within the court system or foster care could be free to enjoy a group home in a natural setting. Tanner helped make that dream come true."

"What a wonderful gift," Nikki replied, aware that Tanner O'Brien had been involved with several charities. She'd done research on the family, long before the boys' ranch had been established.

"Besides the two ranches," Jules continued, "Tanner and his partner own a rodeo stock company. They both competed in rodeo. Tanner retired from bronc riding a year and a half ago, and Dusty McPherson retired from bull riding last year because of injuries. They're on a buying trip right now, mostly for more horses for the boys, but they should be back in a few days. I'll introduce you as soon as they return."

Nikki was disappointed to learn Tanner was gone,

but quickly decided his absence gave her more time to adjust to her new job. She also noticed that Jules hadn't mentioned he'd won the national bronc riding championship before retiring, a sign to Nikki that the O'Briens didn't flaunt their success.

"Are the boys allowed on the Rocking O property?"

"They spend most of their time on the Bent Tree grounds," Jules explained. "They have the run of it, and it's easier to keep an eye on them if they're limited to their own area. We plan to have something once a month with the boys up at our house, such as barbecues when the weather's nice and things like that."

Nikki nodded. "So the boys are more like extended family."

"Very much so," Jules answered as they continued along a wide path. "Of course, you recognized the corral and barn from the main drive. The boys are in classes now, so we won't bother them."

"What kind of classes?"

"They're in the middle of the first semester of school," Jules explained. "The younger boys have on-site teachers, and the older ones mostly participate in a virtual program through our local high school. Tutors are also available to them."

"So they keep up with schoolwork. That's good to hear."

"Education is important."

Nikki nodded in agreement, regretting her own set-aside schooling, and followed as Jules led her across the grounds to several buildings that looked new.

"This is where you'll be living," Jules explained as they stepped through heavy glass doors into the largest of the buildings. A short hall led to a large open room furnished with several sofas and a few tables with chairs. A narrower hallway ran to the right and left of the room. Turning to the right, they walked to the end.

Jules pulled a key out of her pocket and unlocked the door on the left. "It isn't very large and definitely not fancy," she said as she opened the door, then handed Nikki the key, "but you can make it your own however you'd like to."

Stepping inside, Nikki was surprised to see there was so much room. "It's like a little apartment," she said, taking it all in.

"There's a small kitchen back where we came in. We try to keep it well stocked, but if there's something special you want, just let me know. The kitchen facilities here in the building are for staff, although most of your meals will be taken in the boys' dining facility, but feel free to use the kitchen here whenever you like. We have a nurse practitioner on call, and there's a dispensary near the boys' quarters."

"It's wonderful," Nikki said, running her hand along the back of the small sofa.

Jules glanced at her watch, then pointed across the room. "The bedroom is through there."

Nikki started for the door, but stopped when she heard Jules speak to someone. "Would you mind showing Nikki the rest of the ranch?" Jules was saying. "And if you could introduce her to the boys when they're free, I'd appreciate it."

Nikki looked around to see Mac standing in the doorway, studying her, and she quickly looked away. He tended to rattle her nerves.

"Of course," he answered.

Jules gave Nikki an apologetic smile. "I have a conference call scheduled with the licensing board, so I'll leave you in Mac's capable hands."

"I'm sure we'll be fine," Nikki said, her imagination taking flight about what way Mac's hands were capable. Quickly shoving the thought from her mind, she looked at him. If nothing else, working with him would be interesting.

MAC'S FIRST THOUGHT when he'd been introduced to Nikki was that she was too pretty. She appeared to be in her early twenties, with long dark hair, chestnut-brown eyes that tilted up and a generous mouth that belonged on a pixie. She wasn't beautiful in the true sense of the word, and pretty wasn't quite right, either. Whatever it was, he was completely aware of her, and that wasn't something he needed in his life right now.

"Do you want to get settled in first, or would you rather I give you the tour?" he asked.

She didn't even hesitate. "The tour, if you don't mind."

He answered with a nod and motioned for her to follow. "Just so we're all on the same page, this is the administration building, the main building on this part of the ranch."

"Everything is beautiful here. Very different than the eastern part of the state. Are you from Oklahoma?"

"No," he answered. "Back east."

"Are there a lot of ranches there?"

"A few, but my ranching experience was in the western part of the country." Having just met her, he wasn't inclined to offer her any personal information. She'd soon learn that he had the experience necessary for the job.

"This is the commons area," he explained as they

returned to the large room at the center of the building. He quickly pointed out the kitchen, then the office down the hallway in the opposite direction from the living quarters. "The door to the main office is kept locked, but you'll be given a key. You'll find files on the boys there."

"Where do the boys stay?"

"Out this way." He led her down the short hallway and out the door. "There are currently two cabins for them, each able to bed twelve boys, with plans for more in the future."

"The cabins are only for sleeping?" she asked, hurrying to keep up with him.

He shortened his steps. She wasn't an especially short woman, but he stretched beyond six feet. "More like a dormitory," he answered, and gestured toward one of the buildings. "Go ahead and look inside, but only through the windows. The boys don't like adults poking around in their belongings, unless invited."

She took the few steps to the building and leaned forward to peer in a window. For a moment he enjoyed the view. Her dark, straight hair fell forward over slender shoulders. He'd noticed a regal posture when he first saw her standing with Jules near the camp entrance. No slouching for this girl, he'd thought, and she held her head high, looking a person straight in the eye when talking to them. Whether that was natural or she had learned it, he couldn't guess.

She disappeared from view, but within minutes he heard her voice as she rounded the back of the cabin and returned.

"I like that they've personalized their space," she said.

He avoided looking into her brown eyes. "The camp provides them with whatever materials they ask for."

She caught up with him as he walked toward the other buildings. "The O'Briens seem to be very generous."

"They are," he replied, and he was thankful for it. If it hadn't been for Jules, he wasn't sure where he'd be.

"The few people I spoke with in Desperation had good things to say about them. What do you know about the family?"

He'd known Jules since childhood, but didn't feel he needed to mention it. Glancing down at Nikki as she walked beside him, he shrugged. "Very little."

When she didn't ask anything more, he continued around the grounds, showing her the indoor-outdoor dining area, complete with a large industrial kitchen, before pointing out the building where the boys were currently in class.

"Do any of the teachers live on site?" she asked.

"None at present."

"What about counselors?"

He shook his head. "Perhaps in the future, but for now it's a day job, although there's room for another four in the main building."

Her steps slowed and she looked up at him. "We're the only ones living in the main building?"

Her eyes had widened. "Unless you have a problem with it?" he asked. When she shook her head with a smile that appeared genuine, he continued. "The pool is over there," he explained, pointing to it. "And the basketball court."

"It's good they have several things to burn off energy."

He silently acknowledged that she knew boys fairly well. "It helps. I suspect riding will, too."

"How soon will I get to meet them?"

Checking his watch, he answered, "About forty-five minutes. They'll break for lunch, and then have counseling sessions today, before classes resume for another two hours."

"How many counselors?"

"Two are currently working with them. Jules sits in on the sessions twice a week and meets with the counselors every Friday." He wasn't involved with the counseling, so there was little he knew about them, but he realized it might help to clarify his job at the ranch. "Unlike you, I don't have experience working with young boys. My job is to take care of the horses and keep Tanner updated on their health, temperament and what we might need in the future. Jules is the one you should speak with about the boys."

"I'll keep that in mind."

As they returned to the main building, both of them were silent. Leading her to the side door, he stopped and held it open for her.

"How many boys are here?" she asked when they came to the door of her apartment.

"Six."

"That's all?"

"I've been told there will be two or three more arriving later this month. You're free to check out the horses in the barn on your own. If you have any questions, I'll either be in my apartment or in the barn."

"Which is your apartment?" she asked, looking down the hallway in the opposite direction.

"That one." He pointed across from them, the doors of the two rooms facing each other. He sensed that an explanation might be needed. "These rooms are closest to the cabins."

She frowned, but nodded. "That makes sense. And thank you for the tour."

When she held out her hand, he took it and found it to be warm, with a firm grip. He had to remind himself that he'd left his family's marketing firm in Boston confused about his past and his future. No flings, no involvements, no attachments until he discovered who he really was and what he should do with the rest of his life. Jules and Tanner understood that his job at the Bent Tree was only temporary, but even he didn't know for how long.

NIKKI'S KNEES WERE a little weak as she sank to the easy chair in the sitting room of her tiny apartment. She had vowed at a young age never to be taken in by good looks. But she would have had to be blind not to notice that Mac was a very attractive man, although she wouldn't have called him the ranching type. Still, he was definitely stunning, in an arrogant and smooth sort of way. There was a cool detachment about him, more polished than the men she'd met, and—

She slammed her hands down on the arms of the chair and shoved to her feet. Enough! She might have to work with him and live in the same building, but that didn't mean she had to be distracted by him. There were other, more important things she needed to focus on.

Checking her watch, she saw she had time to either take a look at the horses or decide what could be done with her apartment. Because she hadn't even taken a peek at her bedroom, she decided to wait until later to get acquainted with the stock. By waiting, maybe she would get lucky and miss running into Mac.

She opened the door Jules had pointed to and

discovered a small room with a single bed and a bed-side table. To her delight, the wall next to the door was devoted to closet space, with shelves for foldable clothes. Not that she needed a lot of room. Her clothing consisted of jeans and tops, with two or three dresses thrown in for special occasions, which were rare.

The bathroom was tiny, but every inch of space had been utilized with shelves and cupboards for personal items. The shower was roomy enough, and she made plans to take a long, hot one when the day came to an end.

Hearing a knock on her door, she hurried to open it and found Mac waiting in the hallway.

"The boys are out of classes early and ready to meet you." His gaze skimmed over her, sending tiny shocks through her, but his expression revealed nothing of his thoughts and neither did his eyes.

Eager to meet the boys and be around others, she stepped into the hallway, pulling the door shut behind her and locking it before following Mac. They walked silently to the outdoor dining area, where she could see six boys of various ages standing near a long table. As she and Mac drew closer, she saw that the table held trays of double-decker sandwiches and fresh vegetables and fruit, along with two large pitchers of milk.

"Boys," Mac called to them. Four of the six turned to look at him, while the other two continued to pile their plates high, laughing and talking. "All of you," he said more sharply.

The two boys stilled, then turned slowly, wide smiles on their faces. "Mr. Mac," the taller of the two said, and raised his hand in a salute.

Glancing at Mac, Nikki saw him nod and noticed he still wasn't smiling. Did he ever? Did it matter? Not to her, but it might to the boys. The two boys' smiles had dimmed, but they didn't seem to be affected by Mac's chilly attitude. She was also aware that the boy who had spoken was looking her up and down. She ignored it. Boys would always be boys.

"This is Miss Johannson," Mac told them. "She's your new housemother. Please show her the respect she deserves."

"Hi," she said when no one spoke.

"She's an Indian," one of the other boys said.

"Native American," another said. "So what? I am, too. Well, half, anyway."

Nikki smiled, hoping it wouldn't take long to win their trust. "And so am I. My name is Nioka, but you can all call me Nikki. I'll also be teaching you all how to ride." She noted that they stood watching her closely and obviously needed some prodding. "Now it's your turn to tell me your names."

"I'm Billy Norton, and I'm twelve," said the one who was half Native American.

"Hi, Billy," she answered with a smile, which he returned with a friendly one. He was slim, with straight dark hair and dark eyes, and she guessed he wasn't shy in any way.

When none of the others spoke, he jabbed the boy next to him with an elbow. "Your turn," she heard him whisper.

"Ray Stewart," said the second boy, giving Billy a quelling glance.

"How old are you, Ray?" she asked.

"Eleven last week."

"We had a party," one of the other boys added.

"Then happy birthday a little late, Ray." He seemed

more like the quiet type than Billy, but didn't have a problem being a little younger.

She looked at the next boy, one of the two who had waved at Mac. "And what's your name?"

"Shamar Jackson," he answered, pride in his dark eyes.

"How old are you, Shamar?"

"Thirteen."

There was the hint of a swagger, and she smiled to herself. "Officially a teenager, then. Is that cool?"

He ducked his head and then raised it to grin at her. "Yeah. It's cool."

"And you?" she asked the one who had spoken to Mac first.

"Benito Martinez. Fifteen." His chin went up as he met her gaze full-on. "And I don't like horses."

"That's all right," she told him. "Not everyone does. What do you like?"

"Basketball."

"I'm Leon Jones," the boy next to him said, claiming her attention before she could comment on Benito's choice of sport. "And I'm fifteen, too."

There was no lift to his chin as there had been with Benito, but she noted a spark of defiance in his dark eyes. She didn't blame him or any of the boys for hard feelings they might have toward adults. She'd known several who'd experienced some of the same things that had led these boys into the court system. For some, it wasn't a pretty world out there. She'd been lucky, even though she'd come from a broken family and hadn't known her father. But she'd never had to fend for herself on the streets, as some of these boys might have.

"And what about you?" she asked the smallest of the

boys, who stood with his head lowered. "What's your name?"

"Kirby," he said without looking up.

"Kirby Miller. He's eight," Ray offered. "He's the youngest."

Kirby stood a little apart from the others, and she wondered if it was his choice or if the others kept their distance. "Do you like horses?" she asked.

He nodded, but still kept his head down. When he finally lifted it, she saw a two-inch horizontal scar across his left cheekbone. "But Mac said no riding yet."

She looked up at Mac standing beside her. He must have read the question in her eyes, because his answer was a shrug. "We're two horses short. As soon as Tanner and Dusty return, we'll have enough so everyone can ride."

"Of course," she answered, and quickly turned away. Looking at him too closely wasn't a good idea. His steely stare felt as if he could see inside her to her secrets. She couldn't risk that. Instead, she flashed the boys a friendly smile, making sure to include Kirby. "Whatever Mac says. He's the boss with the horses. But it's great meeting all of you. I still have to learn the schedule here, but I hope we'll all become good friends."

Mac indicated it was time to leave, and she followed him away from the outdoor dining hall. They hadn't gone far when she felt him touch her arm.

"Don't expect to become friends with all of them," he said, keeping his voice low, "and be careful how much and what kind of friend you become."

She spun around, facing him, angry that he thought she was completely without common sense. "Let's get something straight," she said, more than ready to get this over with. "I've worked with all kinds of children. Little ones, teenagers, boys, girls. Some had similar problems to those these boys have, and I've never had a bit of trouble. I know how to handle them. Maybe *you* should learn how." Turning on her heel, she left him behind, not caring what he might have to say.

Hoping he wouldn't follow her, she tried to calm herself by taking the long way back to the main building. If there was anything else he wanted to say to her, it could wait. Maybe she shouldn't have been so sharp with him, but it didn't matter what he thought of her. She was here to help boys who hadn't had the advantages in life most kids did, not get involved in a relationship. Her job had to be her main focus, even more important than what had initially brought her here.

When she'd read about the Bent Tree Boys Ranch in a newspaper article, she knew she had to apply for a job. Jules O'Brien had apparently been impressed enough to hire her, and she'd liked Jules from the moment she'd met her. But it was Jules's husband she was more interested in meeting. From the little her mother had told her, Tanner O'Brien was the older of the two brothers she'd never known.

Chapter Two

"So what do you think of Nikki?"

Sitting at the O'Briens' kitchen table that afternoon, Mac looked up from the depths of his coffee cup to see Jules standing at the sink. "If you think she's qualified, why should I question it?"

Shaking her head, Jules sighed, but added a smile. "That's not what I asked you."

He shrugged and returned to stare at the dark brew before him. When he heard a chair slide on the floor, he didn't bother to look up, knowing that Jules had joined him at the table. He also knew it meant she expected an answer. "I guess I don't think anything."

"Oh, come on, Mac. You can't tell me that you missed how pretty she is," Jules teased. "I know you better than that."

Mac gave in, leaning back in his chair and meeting Jules's gaze. "You do know me, maybe too well. But it doesn't mean—"

"I didn't ask if you'd fallen head over heels for her like you did with Missy Templeton when we were nine."

Mac laughed. "You aren't ever going to let me forget about that, are you?"

"Not on your life."

Mac returned his attention to his coffee. "You did check out her credentials, right?"

"Nikki's?" Jules asked. "Of course I did, and I was impressed. Not only does she know horses, she's worked with troubled children. She's had a taste of what some of the boys have lived with." When Mac had no response, she continued. "You and I were lucky, Mac. We had two parents who cared about us and provided us with things others only dream of having."

"Or three parents," he muttered. He felt a hand on his and looked up to see her watching him, a worried frown on her face. "Sorry, it's just on my mind a lot lately."

She gave his hand a squeeze, and then released it. "I know that learning you were adopted by your dad and that he isn't your biological father was a shock, but it doesn't change anything."

"It changed *me*." He couldn't look at her, even though she was the one person he knew he could trust. They'd known each other since they were seven years old, and she was like a sister to him and to Megan, his younger sister. But he still had trouble talking about how his parents had deceived him most of his life, turning that life upside down and leading him to where he was now.

"You're still the same great guy I've always known," Jules said, her voice soft and comforting. "A smart little boy who used to tease me and his sister unmercifully, until poor Megan was in tears, but who grew up to be a very intelligent and caring man."

He looked at her and saw a smile of childhood bliss, and he smiled, too, at the memories. "I'm glad I came here. You were always the sensible one."

"I'm glad you did, too, and I hope you stay for a long time."

He pushed back his chair and stood. "I've wasted

enough of your time," he said, moving to the door. "We both have things to do." But before he could walk out of the room, he stopped and turned back. "Thank you again, both you and Tanner, for giving me the job and a chance to figure out who I am."

Jules shrugged. "We're the ones who are thankful. Just be nice to Nikki, okay?"

Nodding, he slipped out, too many things on his mind to worry about a pretty girl. She might be the perfect distraction, but he wasn't the kind of man to use women that way. The more he worried about his life and his future, the more confused he became. Had he been wrong to leave a very lucrative career when he learned he'd been lied to? He didn't think so. But he still had doubts.

When his chores were finished, Mac chose to visit the kitchen in the main building, to enjoy his meal with some television. Or so he thought, until he discovered Nikki in the small kitchen, bent to examine the contents of the refrigerator. The view she provided wasn't at all unattractive and definitely beat whatever was on the tube that evening.

"Hungry?" he asked, not really interested in conversation.

She jumped at the sound of his voice and faced him. "I didn't know anyone was here."

He took a step back, giving her more space. "I thought you'd be having dinner with the boys, since you're the housemother."

"I thought it would be a good time to unload my belongings from my car," she answered with a shrug. "I cleared it with Jules." She closed the refrigerator, her hands empty, then stepped around him and out the door.

"Aren't you going to eat?" he called to her as she

headed toward the main entrance. Having been raised to be a gentleman, he followed her and searched in the evening's half-light to find her unlocking the door to an older Chevy.

"Is this all you have?" he asked when he caught up with her. There weren't even ten boxes in all, along with a large suitcase.

She turned, one of the boxes in her arms. "Do I need more?"

"You need what you need. It's simply that—" He shook his head. Not that he cared, but there was no reason he couldn't be a gentleman and help her. "Never mind. Give me the box. You can take the smaller one."

She hesitated for a moment, then handed him the box before turning to get another. "Just set it outside the door of my room."

He did, and they didn't speak again until the car was unloaded.

When they were finished, she turned to him. "Thank you for helping," she told him. "It made less work for me. I can get the rest."

"Are you sure?" He leaned his shoulder against the wall, while she attempted to open her door. Noting that she was having some difficulty with her key, he gently took it from her, their hands brushing in the exchange. He felt warmth from only the whisper of the touch and quickly reminded himself that it was simply chemistry between a male and female. It meant nothing, but he wondered if she'd felt it, too.

"Tell me where you want the boxes," he said, opening the door and handing her the key.

She hesitated as if he'd offered more than a little help. "You don't have to do this," she said.

Picking up the first of the boxes, he shrugged. "I don't have anything else do to." It wasn't a lie. Spending the evening alone watching boring television programs that he didn't care about suddenly didn't appeal to him at all.

"Over there is fine." She pointed to a corner near the sofa, then stepped outside the room to grab the suitcase, which she took to the bedroom. Reappearing immediately, she lowered herself to the floor and began opening the first box, while he brought in the others.

When he'd carried all the boxes into the room, he watched as she pulled out a large pottery vase. "Was it hard choosing?" he asked.

She looked up at him from her place on the floor. "Choosing?"

"What to bring."

He barely heard her low-throated chuckle, and then she looked up with a slight smile. "This is it," she said, spreading her arms to indicate the boxes. "This is everything."

He was surprised. The boxes weren't large and couldn't hold much. There weren't even a dozen of them. "You weren't allowed to keep much where you last lived?"

She shrugged. "I've moved around quite a bit."

He nodded. "Too much trucking it all back and forth."

She went back to her unpacking. "Something like that."

"That vase," he said, pointing to the one she had taken out. "Is that handmade?"

Nodding, she picked it up again and ran her finger along the design on it. "By my grandmother when she was very young."

"It's beautiful."

"She loved making pottery."

"Did she teach you how?"

"Yes, but I'm not nearly as good as she was." Gently placing it aside, she then pulled out a polished wood carving of a horse and held it out to him. "My grandfather made this not long before he died."

Mac took it from her and admired the perfection of it. He knew enough about art to appreciate it. The wood was obviously hand polished and glowed in the artificial light in the room. It was as smooth as satin and warm to the touch. "This is priceless." He glanced at her. "But, of course, you know that."

"He liked jewelry making better," she replied, taking the carving and setting it behind her. "Silver, of course."

"And turquoise? Like your ring?" He pointed to her right hand.

She nodded. "Whatever was available, but he often painted pictures on them, instead. Belt buckles, earrings, bracelets. I have a few, if you'd like to see them sometime. The Cherokee take pride in their artistry."

"I'd like that," he replied. "Did you live on the reservation?"

Shaking her head, she looked up at him. "There is no reservation. Those were disestablished years ago."

"Disestablished?" he asked.

"Done away with," she said with a shrug, and went back to her unpacking.

Feeling he was no longer needed, he stepped back. "I'll let you get your unpacking done."

Tilting her head to the side, she studied him. "Thanks for helping." Then she turned her attention to the boxes.

He left quietly, closing the door behind him, and went to the kitchen, but his mind didn't stray far from her while he fixed a sandwich. He couldn't deny the attraction he felt. He couldn't explain it, either. Pretty or not, she wasn't his type. He'd always preferred the more sophisticated, and there was nothing like that about Nikki Johannson. In fact, she was the antithesis of a sophisticate. But still...

"It's nothing serious," he told himself as he walked into his apartment. The attraction was fleeting and wouldn't last. Until then, he'd do as Jules asked and be nice to her, but that was all.

"Do you have the list?" Mac stood at the passenger door of the pickup and waited until Nikki nodded before closing it.

She watched him walk around the front, then she turned to look out her window as he climbed inside. She wanted to tell him that he didn't need to help her into the truck—she could do it fine on her own—but she suspected it wouldn't make any difference. He seemed to be the kind of man who did it automatically.

Leaning back in the seat, she tried to enjoy the drive into Desperation. But even the fall colors of the country-side couldn't distract her thoughts. How did a man like Mac come to work as a ranch hand in Oklahoma? He wore blue jeans, but no Western-style shirts. Instead of even a T-shirt, he wore knit sport shirts. Glancing at his foot on the accelerator, she wondered where he bought his boots. Most stores in Oklahoma sold traditional cowboy boots, but Mac's weren't traditional. His were round toed, not pointed, and without the common angled heel of cowboy boots. Even the leather was smooth. And she had never seen him wear a hat over his longish, light brown hair, much less a Stetson.

No, he wasn't a cowboy, but she had watched him work with the stock the day before, and there was no doubt in her mind that he knew horses. Whether he knew boys or not remained to be seen.

"Have you thought about when you want to start the boys' riding lessons?"

Nikki jumped at the sound of his voice, then shrugged in answer to his question. "Being short on horses presents a problem, but I've been thinking it might be best to start with the basics."

"Such as?" he asked, glancing at her.

"Saddling a horse, first of all. Just being around one, too."

"You're right. The boys are pretty green," he agreed. "Teach the basics first, before they ever climb on an animal."

"Any idea when the new horses will be here?"

"Tomorrow or the next day would be my guess."

Nodding, Nikki was hesitant to dive into something Mac, as head wrangler, might not approve of, but if she wanted to get started, now was the time. "Maybe I can start this afternoon."

"Whenever you're ready."

Surprised that he didn't argue, she smiled. "I'll only need one horse today, and I'll leave the choice to you." But Mac simply nodded in answer, and she chalked it up to whatever burr was under his saddle.

As they approached the edge of town, Mac pulled up to the local grain elevator and backed the pickup to a loading dock. Nikki climbed out immediately, removing any chance for him to come around and open the door for her. They were working, so it wasn't time for his gallantry, if it ever was, and she didn't want anyone in the town of Desperation to think she was some kind of debutante. Not that one look at her would give anyone that idea.

A man who appeared to be in his late fifties and was dressed in jeans, real cowboy boots and a blue work shirt came out of the office and joined them on the dock. "Morning, Mac," he said, glancing at Nikki.

Mac must have noticed, because he turned to her. "Nikki, this is Tom Hastings. He runs the place, so if you ever need anything here, talk to him. Tom, this is Nikki Johannson, the Bent Tree's new housemother and riding instructor."

"Pleased to meet you, miss," the man said, flashing her a smile.

"Nice to meet you, too, Mr. Hastings," Nikki answered.

"Call me Tom. Mr. Hastings is my father." He turned back to Mac. "How many horses you got out there, Mac? Jules wasn't sure how much grain you might need, especially with the grass still a bit green."

"Five horses right now," Mac said, and followed him into the warehouse. "Jules likes to have extra, and what's in the bin is getting low."

Nikki lengthened her stride to keep up with the men and stepped into the chilly, semidark warehouse, where the smell of bagged grain greeted her. She was glad she'd chosen to wear a long-sleeved shirt. Too much grain dust kicked up her allergies and made her skin itch.

"Tanner and Dusty will be back with a few more horses soon," Mac was saying to Tom, "but I don't know how many they'll be bringing with them."

"I heard they were headed for a sale in New Mexico," Tom answered before climbing on a forklift. "I'd say maybe twenty bags for now? You can always get more later if you need it. The O'Briens have always been good to their stock. If it's too much, it can be saved or you can bring it back."

"Twenty sounds good for now," Mac agreed. He motioned for Nikki to follow him, and they returned to the loading dock.

She climbed into the bed of the truck to wait for Tom. When he drove the forklift out onto the dock, she worked with Mac, restacking the fifty-pound bags. It wasn't long before Tom returned with the last load, and she and Mac finished the job quickly.

"Where to now?" Mac asked Nikki as they drove away.

She pulled the list from her pocket and unfolded it. "Cinnamon rolls?"

"The Chick-a-Lick, then."

She looked at him as he started for the main street. "Chick-a-Lick?"

He nodded. "Desperation's café." He turned to look at her. "Do you like cinnamon rolls?"

"Doesn't everybody?" she asked with a grin.

"Then you won't be disappointed in these."

Nikki stared out the window as they drove into the main part of town. It had been years since she'd been in Desperation. But before arriving at the Bent Tree to apply for the housemother job, she'd stopped in the small town and had immediately liked it.

Main Street in Desperation wasn't much different than other small towns, with buildings of varied architecture and color snuggled next to each other. It was a pretty town, clean and well taken care of, as if the people there loved it. Somehow she'd missed seeing the café, but she'd enjoyed a pleasant hour in the Sweet & Yummy Ice

Cream Parlor, one of several businesses housed in the historic old opera house. She'd been impressed with the renovations that had been done to the entire building.

People she'd encountered while enjoying her ice cream had been friendly and open, encouraging her to visit again, as had those she'd asked for directions to the O'Brien ranch. She hoped she would be in the area long enough to consider it home. But that was something she couldn't count on.

She turned her attention to their destination as Mac pulled into a diagonal parking space in front of a building proclaiming it was the Chick-a-Lick Café. Nikki again quickly got out of the truck. He met her at the front and they stepped up onto the sidewalk together.

"Dusty McPherson's wife, Kate, makes the rolls and desserts they sell here," he explained, opening the door of the café for her and letting her pass inside. "She's a good friend of the O'Briens."

"And this Dusty is Tanner O'Brien's partner?"

"They own a rodeo stock company," Mac said, his voice lowered, once they were inside.

Although Nikki hadn't learned a lot when researching the O'Brien family, she did know that she and Tanner shared the same parents. But while he had known his father, she hadn't. Her mother hadn't talked freely about her marriage to Brody O'Brien, only that she'd been far too young to get married and, even more, to start a family. That revelation hadn't come until Nikki was in her teens and had begged her mother for years for information. Even her grandmother was tight-lipped about it.

"Nikki, this is Darla," Mac said as they reached the counter, and introduced her to the young woman behind it. "Nikki is the new housemother and riding instructor at the boys' ranch."

A voice from the other side of the room reached them. "Some people don't want those good-for-nothing boys anywhere near our town."

"Ignore them," Darla whispered.

Nikki greeted her, and while Mac gave the order, she looked around the café. It was typical small town, with several tables and a few booths along the walls. The long counter ran the depth of the room from front to back, with the cash register near the door. Two customers were sitting in a booth, both scowling, and another man sat on one of the swivel stools at the counter. She noticed he was looking at her.

"Don't mind those two old biddies," he said, waving a hand at the booth. When she smiled at him, he nodded. "You're new in town."

"Just this week," she answered.

"You working at the boys' ranch?"

"I've just begun, but I hope to stay a while."

"Well, now, you couldn't ask for a better family to work for. Tanner and Jules are good people, and so are Rowdy and Bridey."

"I've only met Jules," she explained.

"That's right," he said, slapping his hand on his thigh. "Tanner and Dusty are off to a horse sale. You'll meet the others soon enough, and I'd bet my life that you like them."

"I'm sure I will, if they're anything like Jules."

On the other side of her Mac took two big boxes from Darla and joined them. "Rowdy is the Rocking O ranch foreman. Bridey is Tanner's aunt and the one who stocks the refrigerator for us."

"I'll have to remember to thank her." She turned

to Darla. "It was nice meeting you. Both of you," she added, turning to the man.

"You, too, Nikki," Darla said, "and I'm sure we'll see a lot of each other. Jules could get the rolls and desserts cheaper if she'd go directly through Kate, but she likes to help keep us in business."

"You do fine," the man said. "Not another town around has a café as popular as this place." Turning to Nikki, he touched the brim of his gimme cap, emblazoned with the name of a hybrid wheat brand. "Gerald Barnes. If you need anything, you just let me know. I've lived here all my life and will probably die here. Suits me just fine."

Nikki smiled and thanked him, then followed Mac outside. "They're nice people," she said, climbing into the truck and closing the door.

Mac set the boxes between them and then settled behind the steering wheel, his mouth pulled down in a deep frown. "Desperation has a lot of nice people, in spite of a few who have their own opinions about the boys at the ranch."

As he pulled away from the curb and headed the pickup down the street, Nikki wondered if she might be able to get some idea of how people in Desperation felt about her mother. If most, like Gerald Barnes, had lived there all their lives, someone had to remember her. Nikki hoped what they remembered wasn't as bad as she suspected it might be. Sally Rains O'Brien had been a wild child, something Nikki knew her mother still regretted.

LEANING AGAINST the top rail of the fence surrounding the corral, Mac watched and listened. He hoped Nikki wasn't as nervous as he was about this first riding lesson.

These weren't simple schoolboys. Some of them had been in trouble with the law, and some of them came from troubled homes. Inexperienced with boys, he hadn't spent a lot of time with them, although he'd been at the ranch a week before they'd arrived two weeks ago. Jules and Bridey had watched over them before Nikki had been hired. There hadn't been a lot of time for Nikki to spend with the horses, either, but from what he could tell, she knew what she was doing.

Nikki stood in the middle of the enclosure with the gentlest of the horses. The chestnut mare stayed steady as Nikki walked around her, pointing out the different areas of the horse.

"When are we going to ride?" Billy asked.

She gave him a smile that would have melted any boy's heart. "It may be slow going for you for a while, Billy. I know you've spent time with horses, but I'd like to start with the basics for the others. The more we know about horses, the better we can ride them. Don't you agree?"

It was clear that Billy was disappointed, but after a quick duck of his head he looked up to smile at her. "Yeah."

Mac was impressed by the way she stuck to the basics, while somehow making it interesting, even for him. The boys seemed to hang on her every word, watching how she touched the animal, handling the mare with respect. He knew from his own experience that treating a horse well—whether it was a Thoroughbred, a quarter horse or even a mule—would bring out the best, not only in the horse, but in the rider.

He watched as she demonstrated how to approach a horse, how and where to stroke it and even how to give a carrot treat without the risk of a finger getting in the way. Even Leon and Benito, who found everything either dull and boring or beneath them, seemed fascinated.

"Do you know any tricks?" Kirby asked.

Nikki turned to him, her smile softer with him than with any of the others. "A few."

"Will you teach us some?" Leon asked.

"When you and your horse are ready."

"When we have enough horses, you mean," Benito added, the disgust in his voice clear even to Mac.

She glanced at Mac before answering Benito. "They may arrive this weekend, so it won't be long."

His frown deepened. "We been here for two weeks."

Not meaning to, Mac tensed. Benito's belligerence could escalate, and he doubted Nikki was prepared for it. He didn't want to alarm her by stepping in, but he wanted to be ready the second it appeared she couldn't handle it.

"You've been feeding the horses, right?" she asked.

"Yeah, every day," the boy grumbled.

"And you think you're ready to ride?"

Even standing still, there was a swagger to him. "Sure. Why not?"

"Then go get a saddle."

For a second Benito stared at her, then he strode to the barn.

She turned back to the others, who showed more interest in watching Benito's exit than hearing instructions about grooming. Mac wasn't sure what to think. The mare might stand still to have a saddle thrown on, but beyond that, there was no telling what would happen if Benito tried to mount.

When Benito emerged, it was obvious the nearly grown boy was struggling a bit under the weight of the saddle. When he reached Nikki, he dropped it at her feet.

She stood away from the other boys and leaned closer to Benito, but Mac didn't hear what she said. Benito's head snapped up and he stared at her again. Mac held his breath. But instead of anything unfortunate happening, Benito turned for the barn again.

Nikki continued with her instructions until Benito reappeared, a saddle blanket and a bit with reins in his hands. "That's great," she told him. "Go ahead and saddle her."

"But—" For a brief moment his bravado disappeared, then he planted his feet apart in the dirt, stuck his chin out in defiance and confronted her. "You know I don't know how."

"Which is why we're here." Her tone was matter-of-fact, and her smile was sincere. "You all may think riding a horse is nothing more than getting on and riding away, but there are still many things to learn."

Mac gripped the fence in front of him, ready to intervene.

"How's she doing?"

He hesitated to turn to look at Jules, who had walked up to stand beside him, and barely glanced at her before focusing on the activity in the corral. "We'll know in a few seconds."

"Benito can be a handful," Jules said, obviously having sized up the situation.

Mac didn't hear what Nikki said to the boy, but his stance immediately relaxed. So did Mac. "She's doing okay," he said as he watched Benito shrug and back away.

Jules propped her arms on a fence rail. "It appears she is. I had a feeling she would."

"You had more faith than I did," he grudgingly admitted. But as she'd said, Benito could be a handful, and time would tell if Nikki could continue to hold her own with him.

Jules turned at the sound of her name being called. "Over here, Bridey."

Mac watched as Tanner's aunt joined them. "Ah, the lovely Irishwoman," he greeted her.

Bridey Harcourt harrumphed. "And from a Scotsman, no less." But her bright blue eyes twinkled merrily as they always did when they teased each other. "Is that the new housemother I've been hearing about?" she asked as she moved to stand beside Jules.

"That's her," Jules answered. "What do you think?"

Bridey frowned. "I don't know much about horses, so I've no opinion on that. But boys?" Her face brightened when she smiled again. "That's something I have experience with, and she seems to be getting on with this lot."

They watched while Nikki wrapped up the lesson, sent the boys on their way, then turned to walk toward the fence. "They're eager to start riding," she announced before she reached them.

"Oh, my," Bridey whispered.

"What's wrong?" Jules asked.

"Why, nothing. Just that I—" Bridey shook her head. "I'm sure they're very eager. Boys have so little patience."

"And don't have a lot more as men," Jules added, laughing.

But Bridey's sunny smile looked forced to Mac. Was there something about Nikki's Native American heritage that bothered her? That couldn't be. Not when her nephew and great-nephew were part Cherokee.

As Jules made the introductions, Bridey seemed relaxed, but she watched Nikki closely. Before Mac could give it more thought, Kirby shouted for Nikki. She excused herself and hurried to see what he needed.

"Do the boys like her?" Bridey asked.

"So far she's handling them well," Mac answered.

"Then I hope she stays with us. Jules has enough on her hands, and I'm certain you could use the help, too."

"Especially when we add more boys," Jules agreed. "I think they'll all do better once Tanner and Dusty return with the new horses. It will give the boys something to focus on."

But Mac wasn't listening. He was watching Nikki with Kirby. She had knelt to the boy's level and was talking to him. When she finished, she gave him a hug before standing again and then put an arm around his shoulders. Mac again had to admit she had a flair with the boys. They had all accepted her, more or less, but Kirby was obviously her favorite, and Mac almost felt jealous about the way she easily dealt with the boys.

Chapter Three

Even though it was Saturday and technically her day off, Nikki offered to work. After making sure the boys were occupied when lunch was over, she headed for the main building. It was the perfect time to look over the boys' files and get to know their backgrounds and the reasons they were living at the ranch.

At the door to the office, she pulled out the set of keys Mac had given her. It took two of the keys to get her into the inner office where she found the file cabinet, and she unlocked that with the last of the keys on the ring. Settling on the chair at the small desk, she opened the first file and started reading.

There were moments when she wanted to cry over what she read. In spite of her mother being overprotective and unwilling to share information about the past, her childhood had been full of wonderful memories, and she'd always felt loved by her mother and grandmother. That hadn't been the case for some of the boys. The older ones, Benito and Leon, were at the ranch under judges' orders. Both had been involved in petty thefts of some kind, in addition to vandalism, but she suspected even that was based on poor home lives. Benito was the oldest of eight children, and there was a history of domestic violence in the family. Leon's mother was on her fourth husband, with little time for her three sons and daughter.

Nikki sighed as she continued to read. Shamar had lived with an aunt who didn't like being saddled with a boy to raise and had left him to fend for himself much of the time. Ray's parents had vanished, and his older brothers and sisters had taken turns caring for him, but with some of them serving time in jail, he was shuffled back and forth. Billy had been in foster care since he was two, shuttled from one home to another, but never able to bond with anyone.

But it was Kirby's story that brought a tear to her eye. Two years before, his mother had died of pneumonia, leaving him to live with his father. A few months before coming to the Bent Tree, Kirby had been found roaming the streets of Oklahoma City, and his father, who'd claimed despondency over his wife's death, had been charged with neglect. There was still a chance Kirby would be returned to his father, and Nikki sensed that might not be a good thing.

She'd worked in intake at Youth Services and had heard stories that broke her heart. Many of the children she'd worked with had gone on to foster care or to live with relatives. Some had been adopted. She knew there was never a guarantee that life would be better for any of them, and she was grateful for the Bent Tree—one more place for some of them to live and grow.

When she finished reading the last of the files, she rubbed the back of her neck, which ached from sitting too long. Glancing at her watch, she realized it was much later than she'd thought, and she hurried to put things away and lock up again. Knowing the history of the boys and how bad it had been for them, she wanted to do something special. She had an idea, but it would take Mac's help to do it.

She went in search of him and finally found him in the barn, scooping what was left of the grain from the storage bin into the trailer hooked to a garden tractor. "Can I talk to you?" she asked.

Stopping his work, he rested his hands on top of the handle of the grain scoop. "What about?"

Butterflies fluttered in her stomach, and she quickly tried to dismiss the idea that it might be because his eyes looked bluer than ever, or that his shirt, damp with sweat, stuck to him like a second skin. "Could you use some help with that?" she asked.

Shrugging, he handed her the shovel, then reached for another for himself. "Is this what you wanted to talk to me about? Helping?"

She began scooping, thinking of her plan. "Of course not. I want to do something special for the boys."

"Such as?"

"A campfire."

He looked at her. "Campfire?" When she nodded, he blew out a breath.

She worked for several more minutes, avoiding his gaze as he silently watched her.

"What's your problem?" he asked, setting aside the shovel and planting his hands on his hips, his legs spread wide as she rubbed her arms.

"No problem," she answered, switching the grain shovel to her other hand so she could rub that arm. Her allergies were kicking in. The itching was getting worse.

He frowned, watching every move she made, which made her more nervous and caused an even bigger need to scratch. "I'm serious, Nikki. You've been rubbing your arms and legs, and your face has red splotches on it. Not only is it making *me* itch, it isn't at all attractive."

She guessed the last was his attempt at humor, but she didn't smile. Hating to admit a weakness, she knew she had to tell him. "It's the grain dust. I'm allergic to it."

The furrow between his eyes deepened. "Then why did you offer to help?"

She couldn't look him in the eye. "I figured it couldn't hurt."

He took the scoop from her hand. "Next time, just get to the point. What can be done for the itching?"

"A shower should do the trick," she answered.

He nodded. "When do you want to do this campfire thing?"

"Tonight," she answered. "After supper. I'll see if Bridey has some marshmallows they can roast."

He at least seemed to be considering the idea. "All right," he said after a short silence. "I'll get it set up for you, but you'd better make sure you have plenty of marshmallows. One bag isn't going to be enough for those boys."

Pleased that he was willing to help, she hurried to the main building and unlocked the door to her apartment, eager to wash off the offending grain dust.

Inside, she went into her bedroom, where she grabbed fresh clothes on her way to the bathroom.

The spray from the shower was not only cleansing, it was relaxing. When she was done, she stepped out, wrapped herself and her freshly shampooed hair in towels and felt much better. She took her time dressing in clean jeans and a gauzy top with colorful embroidery before drying her long, straight hair.

She checked on the boys again and stopped to watch

the four older ones playing basketball. Kirby and Ray sat on the ground on the far side of the court, intent on the half-court game.

"Are you Nikki?"

She turned, shading her eyes with her hand against the late-afternoon sun to see an older boy she guessed to be about seventeen or eighteen walking toward her. "Yes, I'm Nikki."

"I'm Shawn. Tanner's my uncle," he said as he came to a stop in front of her. "I've been staying with a friend in town while we worked on a science project."

Her breath caught. Tucker's son? She hadn't been able to find much information on the younger of her two brothers and hoped Shawn wouldn't notice her surprise or that she was near tears. "It's nice to meet you, Shawn," she said, doing her best to keep her voice friendly without going overboard. "I was just getting ready to go up to the house to find Bridey."

"Aunt Bridey and Jules went into town. Can I help with something?"

She shook her head, disappointed that she wouldn't be able to ask Bridey about the marshmallows. "Probably not. We're having a campfire after supper tonight, and I was going to ask if there were any marshmallows. If Mac won't mind keeping an eye on the boys, maybe I can run into town to get some."

"You don't need to," Shawn assured her. "I'll go call them and ask them to bring back a few bags."

Nikki couldn't have been happier. "That would be great, if it isn't too much trouble."

"No trouble."

"Would you like to join us tonight?"

"Thanks, but I only stopped at home to get some supplies for our project. And I need to get going as soon as I call Jules and let her know about the marshmallows."

Nikki nodded and thanked him for his help, then forced herself to turn back to the boys, instead of waiting for her nephew—her nephew!—to walk away. "Hey, guys!" she shouted over the whoops and hollers of their basketball game. "Make sure you listen for the supper bell and are on time. When we've finished eating, we'll meet in the circle of trees."

When she was certain they'd all heard her, she started for the main building. She hoped Mac didn't mind setting up the campfire, but she felt sure if he needed her help, he'd ask for it.

Jules had already planned to share the supper with the boys, so Nikki was on her own. Stopping in the kitchen, Nikki made a sandwich and took it back to her room, eating it while she worked on a riding schedule. She'd just finished when there was a knock on her door. Opening it, she found Mac.

"I'll be right out to help with the campfire," she told him.

"You don't need to. It's almost ready. You can start as soon as I get the fire going." He glanced at his watch. "Shouldn't be too long."

"You're joining us, right?" she asked. "I mean, after all, you've done all of the work, and I'm sure the boys would like it if you're there."

"I suppose I can." He raked his gaze over her. "With the sun down, there's a chill in the air. A jacket might be a good idea."

She watched him walk away. She would have to find a way to ignore his long glances. Her skin had prickled with that one, and she couldn't blame it on grain dust.

"ARE YOU SURE there isn't something I can do to help?"

Mac looked up from the fire he was tending to find Nikki standing beside him. With a nod of his head, he indicated a large pile of firewood several yards away. "You can grab another log or two."

He was tempted to watch her walk away, but decided he should try to curb that kind of urge, and focused on the fire instead. Give it another week, he told himself. By then there'd be something he didn't like about her, and she'd be out of his system.

"I see you brought some straw bales," she said from behind him.

He turned, took the armload of logs she held and placed them on the small blaze. "I don't want the boys getting too close to the fire."

"Good idea, and the bales will keep them off the cold ground. But you've gone to a lot of work. I should have been out here helping."

Shrugging, he moved away a few steps. Whatever perfume she was wearing was enticing, and he knew better than to let that distract him. "You had things to do. I was free." He hadn't minded the extra work, but he wouldn't tell her that. She might think he was open to helping with the boys whenever the whim struck her. He wasn't. He didn't know how to relate to them, and it wasn't his job to know. He'd stick with what he knew—horses.

Once the blaze was going well, the boys began to appear. First Kirby hurried to claim the space next to Nikki, followed by Ray, his bunk mate, who chose the bale next to them. Billy scooted in by himself and chose to sit with Ray. To keep the bales far enough from the fire, Mac had spaced them a few feet apart. He also hoped it would keep the poking and punching between the boys to a minimum. He hadn't forgotten what it was like to be a boy at that age.

After Shamar and Leon arrived to claim the last bale, Benito trailed in and took the empty spot beside Mac, who had a clear view of the younger boys; the older ones were within reach, just in case they decided to play some tricks.

With Nikki there, Mac hoped the boys would all be on their best behavior.

The marshmallows Bridey had given him were distributed, along with the sticks he'd found, and the boys settled in, telling the usual horror tales of clawed hands on door handles and missing teens. Across from Mac, Kirby huddled against Nikki, his eyes wide, while the firelight threw eerie shadows across his dark face. Watching them, Mac wondered if Kirby's growing attachment to her was wise, but then it wasn't his problem either way.

He turned to Benito beside him, knowing he couldn't sit there in silence. "How are you getting along with Nikki?"

The boy shrugged his broad shoulders. "She's okay."

"I noticed she kind of showed you that there are still things left to learn before getting on a horse."

Benito was silent for a moment. "I just figured you got on, kicked the horse and off you rode. That's how they do it in the movies."

"And the bad guy always loses in the movies," Mac pointed out. "But movies aren't real life."

The nearly grown boy turned and looked him square in the eye. "That's easy for you to say."

Mac had no reply. He'd had nearly everything he'd

ever wanted. The best education, two parents who loved him, and wealth. What had Benito had?

The fire began to die down along with the conversation, and Mac decided it was time to call it a night. "Shamar," he called to the biggest of the group, "help me move these bales under the trees, while the rest of the boys clean up the area."

Shamar grumbled, but did as he was asked. When he and Mac were away from the others, he turned to him. "How come you picked me to do this? Don't like the color of my skin?"

Mac pointed to the boy's chest. "Your shirt says 'Mr. Awesome.' I thought you'd be the best man for the job."

Shamar stared at him. "It's a T-shirt, man."

"Billboard of the century, they say," Mac answered with a shrug. "Now, are you going to show me how awesome you are and help with the rest of the bales?"

Turning around to see what the others were doing, Shamar grunted. "It beats picking up sticks and trash."

By the time they finished with the bales, the area was cleaner than it had been when they'd begun the evening, and the boys were beginning to wander back to their bunkhouses. Mac tossed the dirt he'd dug up earlier onto the fire, stirred the embers with a shovel to make sure there weren't any live ones, then poured water from a bucket on it all, stirring again, until he was sure everything was cool. With shovel and bucket in hand, he looked around and saw that everyone was gone.

After stowing the campfire gear, he headed for his apartment and let himself inside. His sitting room was quiet, and he suddenly felt at loose ends. With Tanner and Dusty gone, Jules had been the only one around to talk to, but she had her own work and her family, and he didn't want to bother her. She and Tanner had done enough for him already.

As he was straightening a painting of the Thames he'd purchased on a trip to Great Britain, he felt the presence of someone. Turning, he saw Nikki standing at his open doorway. He'd forgotten to close the door.

"You brought your own furniture," she said. "It's very nice."

Should he ask her in? He couldn't decide. It might only fuel his attraction to her. But he also knew a gentleman would at least offer.

Before he could decide, she'd moved across the hall to her door. "I'll see you tomorrow," she told him, her hand on the doorknob. "Thank you for helping."

He didn't have a chance to reply before she ducked inside her apartment.

He stood in his doorway, wondering what she was all about. He was tempted to get to know her better, but if he didn't know himself, as he once had, how could he even think of getting to know someone else?

NIKKI PUSHED AWAY from the breakfast table the next morning and stood, surveying the sleepy faces of the boys. "I want to see all of you at the corral in ten minutes," she told them as they finished their breakfast.

"But it's Sunday," Benito reminded her. "We were going to play basketball."

"You can do that this afternoon," she answered. "I'll see you all in ten minutes, no more."

She hadn't slept well. Her dreams had been of a tall man with baby-blue eyes—a man she didn't want to identify, and she shook her head to clear the cobwebs that even a shower hadn't washed away. Shivering in the early-morning chill, she gathered the equipment she would need. The remnants of her dreams would vanish as soon as she started the day's lesson.

When she entered the corral, she was greeted by the smiles of six boys. Nothing could beat that.

Instead of a using a real horse for the day's lesson, she'd found an old saddle frame in the storage room of the barn. To make it the right height, she'd asked Mac to set it on concrete blocks. Only after all the boys mastered saddling the wooden "horse" would she allow them to try the real thing. She was confident it wouldn't be long until that happened.

With all the boys gathered around the makeshift mount, she waited for the jokes and jabs to subside. "Okay, we've already learned about the parts of the horse and the saddle. Now we're going to put all that together and learn how to saddle a horse."

Shamar looked around the corral. "So where's the horse?"

Everyone laughed, but Nikki remained silent, waiting until they quieted before she went on with the lesson. "I'll show you all how it's done. Watch carefully, and then each of you will get a chance to try it."

With practiced ease she saddled the wooden horse, carefully explaining each step as she went. Until they could handle the saddle correctly on their own, she wouldn't bother with a bridle.

"Who wants to be first?" she asked, her gaze going from boy to boy.

"Let Billy," Leon said. "He already knows how to ride."

She suspected Leon was trying to avoid the possibility of being chosen. "Thanks for volunteering to be first, Leon."

"But I didn't—"

"Go ahead and start."

Leon's mulish expression told her how displeased he was. Nikki didn't care. None of them would get it the first time, but by the second time she had hopes they would have the hang of it.

"One more thing," she said as Leon picked up the saddle blanket. "I'll stop you if you skip a step or do something wrong, and the next person will start from the beginning."

Leon's expression didn't change as he tossed the blanket onto the wooden horse.

"Stop," Nikki said. When Leon turned to stare at her, she merely smiled. "Thanks, you did fine."

"What?" His eyes narrowed. "But what did I do wrong?"

"Watch the next person, and you'll see. You'll learn more quickly by watching, instead of me telling you, I promise."

He shrugged his shoulders and returned to stand with the others. "If you say so."

"Ray," she called, removing the blanket, "why don't you try it next?"

Ray looked at the other boys before reluctantly walking up to the wooden horse.

"Think about it, Ray," Nikki told him. "There are seven steps. You know them. Leon was just a bit eager and didn't think it through. He'll do great next time."

Ray nodded, his expression serious, then he picked up the grooming brush sitting on the corner of one of the cinder blocks. As if the wooden horse was real, he brushed it head to tail.

"That's what I forgot," Leon said.

"You'll remember the next time," Nikki assured him. "Go on, Ray."

Nodding again, this time with a slight smile, Ray placed the saddle blanket properly on the back of the horse, smoothing it down. He turned for the saddle, but looked at Nikki. "I don't know if I can lift it."

"Give it a try. If you can't, one of the others can help you with it."

He managed to pick up the saddle the way she'd shown them. Taking a deep breath, he hefted it high and placed it on the back of the wooden horse.

"Stop," Nikki said.

"Aw, gee," Ray mumbled and returned to stand with the others. His face suddenly brightened. "I remember now."

Benito was next and went through each step, remembering to hook the far stirrup over the saddle horn and the cinch over the saddle seat before placing the saddle on the horse, the easiest part for him. He stood looking at the wooden horse, a perplexed expression on his face. "I forget what's next," he admitted, without his usual defiance, and stepped back to join the others.

Shamar took his turn and made it through the same steps Benito had, then advanced to the next to let the stirrup and cinch down, but he had trouble with the cinch. "Next," he said, when he couldn't get the D ring to work. "My gram would say I'm all thumbs today."

The other boys laughed good-naturedly as Billy walked to the wooden horse to take his turn. "I think I should tell you all something," he said, ducking his head. "I know how to ride, but I've never put a saddle on a horse."

"You'll know how after today," Nikki told him. "And won't that surprise everyone?"

Billy went through each step slowly and finally finished with cinching the saddle. When he was done, he beamed with pride.

"Very good! But there's one thing you all forgot, and I didn't stop you, because I wanted to see if anyone remembered." She turned to Kirby. "Your turn."

"I think he's too tall," Kirby said.

"Who's too tall?" Nikki asked.

He pointed at the wooden horse. "Him. The dummy horse."

Everyone laughed and someone shouted, "Maybe we should name him Dumbbell."

"How about Woody?" another boy suggested.

Nikki smiled. "How about we let Kirby have his turn?"

"Can he use a stepladder?" Shamar asked. "I'm not trying to be mean, but he's going to have problems reaching that high, even to brush it."

"Not a stepladder," Nikki said with a shake of her head, "but if two of you will go inside the barn, you'll find a cinder block like those." She pointed to the stack of blocks where the wooden horse sat. "He can use that. We'll find something better when we're working with a real horse."

Benito and Leon raced to get the cinderblock and returned to set it next to the dummy horse. Kirby climbed onto it and began the first step, slowly and painstakingly. He brushed the horse, then checked to make sure the hair was smooth and lying in the direction of growth. Nikki's heart swelled with pride. It was the one thing the others had forgotten to do.

When he got to the step where he needed to lift the saddle, Shamar joined him. "It's okay?" Shamar asked.

Nikki nodded.

Kirby smoothed the saddle blanket, and Shamar helped him lift the saddle to the back of the horse. Kirby checked that the blanket was smooth on both sides, pulled down the stirrup and cinch, pulled the cinch through, and even with his smaller hands he managed to hook the cinch.

The other boys applauded when he was finished, and so did Nikki. She had saved him for last for a reason. "See? Anybody, no matter how young or small, can learn to saddle a horse. Now, let's do it all over again. Leon, you're first up."

By the second time through, each of the boys was able to saddle the dummy horse quickly and without a mistake. Nikki congratulated them all on passing the test—one of the most important—and promised to join them later for lunch.

They helped put away the saddle, blanket and brush, leaving the wooden horse for the next day, and were headed for their bunkhouses when a shiny blue pickup with a long trailer behind it drove up the lane.

"It's Tanner!" Billy shouted, and ran to meet the truck as it came to a stop near the barn.

Nikki's heart seemed to stop, then resumed to pound in her chest. She could barely breathe. This was the moment she had been waiting for. She would finally get a chance to meet her brother.

Jules came hurrying from the house, a toddler running in front of her. "Daddeeee!" the little boy shouted.

At Nikki's initial interview, Jules had mentioned they had a son, but this was Nikki's first opportunity to see the little boy, and she watched him run to his dad.

When the driver's door of the truck opened, a tall man wearing a black hat scooped up the small boy. As

Jules reached the pair, another man exited the truck on the other side. Nikki wished she'd known more about these people before she'd come to the ranch, but there'd been only so much she could learn without asking questions, and she'd been afraid doing that would raise suspicions.

Tugging on her husband's hand, Jules brought him to where Nikki and the others stood. "I want you to meet someone," she told him, and smiled at Nikki. "Nikki, this is my husband, Tanner O'Brien. Tanner, Nikki Johannson is our new housemother, and she's also teaching the boys to ride."

He touched the brim of his hat with his fingers and smiled. "Pleased to meet you, Nikki."

Nikki tried to calm her galloping heart, and her legs threatened to stop supporting her, but she tried to hide it. "Your wife was very kind to give me the job, Mr. O'Brien," Nikki managed to say, feeling tongue-tied.

"It's Tanner," he said. "We've never stood on ceremony at the Rocking O."

Jules tickled her son's neck with her fingers, making him giggle. "You haven't met Wyoming, have you, Nikki?" she asked.

"No, but it's easy to see he's his daddy's boy," Nikki replied.

"He's two," Jules said, reaching for the little boy, who clung to his daddy's neck and wailed. "Come on, sweetheart," she told him. "Daddy needs to take care of the horses. We'll have our time with him later."

After he'd given her the boy and added a quick kiss, Tanner went around to the back of the trailer to help the other man with the horses. Jules passed Nikki and patted her shoulder, and Nikki was left to watch the man she hadn't known existed until she was thirteen. There was no doubt in her mind that she and Tanner O'Brien shared the same family tree. She longed to tell him who she was, but her mother had warned her not to contact him. She hadn't yet decided if she would risk that and thought it might be best if she waited until he knew her better. Until then, she would remain silent about their kinship, but she hoped with all her heart that someday she could reveal her secret.

Chapter Four

Now that the horses had arrived, the boys talked nonstop about riding. That evening, they all attended a barbecue at the O'Briens' to welcome Tanner home, and the boys were still wound tight from the excitement of the day. Getting them to settle down and go to sleep was proving to be a major chore.

"You'll ask him, won't you?" Billy begged, not for the first time.

"As soon as I can," Nikki answered, knowing he meant Mac. "But it isn't going to happen if you all don't get in your rooms and go to bed."

Ray bounced on his bed, his eyes bright and eager. "Just tell him we can saddle our horses now, so we're ready to *ride*."

Nikki rested her hand gently on his shoulder, hoping she could calm him. "Be patient, Ray. You'll be riding like you've been on a horse all your life soon."

Benito seemed to be the only one who wasn't eager. "But we have more to learn, right?" he asked.

"We do," Nikki answered, remembering his stated preference for basketball.

"It's not like in the movies," he added. "We gotta learn how to do it right."

"Exactly," Nikki agreed. "Now, go on to bed. I'll be in to check on you as soon as these guys are tucked in."

"I don't need to be tucked in," Billy announced.

Nikki hid her smile as she waved the older boys out of the room and turned to Billy. He was the oldest of the three younger boys and often enjoyed his seniority. "Of course you don't. It's just a saying." She waited until he was under the covers, then turned to Kirby in the next bed.

"You can turn out the light now," Kirby said, already in his bed. "We're going to sleep."

"Okay, I'll see you in the morning." She moved to the door and flipped the light switch, bathing the room in darkness. "Sleep tight."

Checking on the other boys, she found them all in bed. Not asleep, but she knew it wouldn't be long before they were. She and Mac had been invited to return to the O'Briens', but before she did, she had one stop to make. She'd intended to make a note of all the boys' birthdays when she was in the office the day before, but she'd forgotten. Fearing she'd forget again, she hurried to the main building and gathered the information she needed.

Just as she stepped into the hallway from the office and turned to walk back to her apartment, she saw a small, dark figure race across the unlit hallway from the kitchen to the main entry hall, a bundle dragging behind him. The building was dark, but not dark enough that she couldn't tell who she'd seen as she heard the quiet *swish* and the *thunk* of the main door opening and closing.

Was she imagining things, or was Kirby stealing food? She'd been positive he was ready to sleep when she left him, but thinking again, she remembered he had seemed eager to get rid of her. *And he knew she was returning to the O'Briens'*. He'd overheard Mac reminding her they were expected when she'd finished putting the boys to bed.

But why would Kirby steal food? Because she didn't know what food Bridey had added, there was no way of knowing what might have been taken—if any had been. She didn't know how long she stood there debating what she should do, but she was certain what she'd seen hadn't been a figment of her imagination.

When the door opened at the other end of the hall, she let out a screech. The lights came on and Mac walked inside, instantly spotting her. "A little jumpy, are we?" he asked.

Her heart thudded in her chest, and she hoped he didn't notice her distraction. Mac unnerved her as it was. She didn't know what to do about it any more than she knew what to do about Kirby. Keeping her eyes and ears open would probably solve the Kirby problem, but Mac was a different story.

"I was in the office," she answered. "I wanted a list of the boys' birthdays."

He stopped a few feet in front of her and studied her closely. "We're all waiting for you. You could have gotten the dates later."

She nodded and took a deep breath before answering. "I didn't want to forget to do it."

"Okay, but we need to get going," he said, taking her arm.

His touch startled her and she looked up at him. "I'm sorry I kept everyone waiting. I didn't think it would take me so long."

"Don't worry about it," he said, leading her out the main doors.

But it wasn't being late to the get-together that worried her. It was Kirby. "Is there some reason we're in a rush?" she asked as she tried to keep up with his long stride.

"Sorry," he said, letting go of her and shortening his steps. "I was beginning to think you were trying to avoid going back."

She wouldn't let on that he was dangerously close to the truth. Being around Tanner made her nervous, but she couldn't hide from him. "Why would I do that?"

"I don't know."

She could feel him watching her in the dark, lit only by a tall yard light, when he slowed his steps. "You aren't nervous about being around the O'Briens without the boys, are you?"

She refused to look at him. "Why would I be afraid?"

"That's what I'm wondering."

"You're imagining things."

Stopping, he turned and placed a hand on her shoulder. "It's not uncommon to feel ill at ease with your employer, especially when you're new."

His touch made her head swim, but she managed to glare at him. "And you know this how?"

"I've been a new employee, that's how."

"And so have I, several times, so if you'll please let go of me…"

She felt his hesitation, but he did as she asked and turned away. Squeezing her eyes shut for a moment, she tried to calm herself. Mac's hands on her had definitely done a number on her heart.

Mac wished he'd kept his mouth shut. *Let that be a lesson,* he thought. *Don't try to help someone who doesn't want help.*

When he turned the corner of the big ranch house to join the others, he could hear the music. "I see you dragged out the oldies but goodies," he said as he and Nikki stepped onto the patio.

"There you are," Jules said, greeting Nikki with a warm smile. "I was afraid you were trying to avoid us or were just too tired to come back."

"The boys weren't eager to settle down," Nikki explained. "They're all sleeping now."

Mac turned to Jules. "I can't believe you're just standing there," he said, feeling the beat of the music. Walking over to her, he took her hand. "Come on, let's show them how to party." When he swept her into his arms, she tipped back her head and laughed. "I'll bet that cowboy doesn't dance with you," he said loudly enough for everyone to hear and nodding at Tanner, who stood watching them with a grin. Nikki, he noticed, was staring, her eyes wide.

"She can two-step with the best of them," Tanner said.

Mac stopped moving. "Texas Two-Step?"

"Hush," Jules said. "We don't call it that here in Oklahoma."

Mac tried for a sober nod and looked over his shoulder at Tanner. "And I suppose you're going to tell me you taught her."

"She's a fast learner," Tanner answered with a wink.

Mac laughed and spun Jules in a circle. "Maybe I should take lessons," he said, handing her off to her husband.

Tanner slipped a hand around his wife's waist. "If you want to stick around these parts, it's the only way to survive."

Turning to Nikki, Mac held out his hand. "Your turn."

She took a step back. "No, I think—I think I'll pass."

"What? You can't dance?" he asked.

She squared her shoulders and looked him in the eye. "Of course I can." But instead of taking his hand as he'd thought she would, she moved away and settled on one of the chairs.

The awkward moment was saved by Bridey, who stepped outside with a tray of dessert glasses. Shawn followed and took a seat near his uncle.

"Let me help," Mac said, hurrying to lend a hand. He took the tray from her and studied the glasses. "There isn't a tiny bit of the devil in these, is there?"

Bridey laughed and pointed to a table. "It's one of Tanner's favorites, but don't have too much, or there'll be the devil to *pay*."

Tanner rubbed his hands together. "Irish Jig Dessert! You haven't made this for years, Bridey."

The woman's face colored with pleasure. "I thought it would be a nice way to welcome Nikki. Come on," she urged everyone, "give it a go."

Shawn jumped from his chair, but his uncle stopped him. "Shawn, I'm not sure you should be having any."

Jules joined them. "Oh, Tanner, it isn't going to hurt him. There's only a little whiskey in it. Let him have a glass."

"Better they have it at home than out with their friends."

Everyone turned to look at Nikki, who ducked her head, obviously wishing she hadn't spoken.

"She's right," Tanner agreed. "I had a few glasses of my own when I was his age." He turned to his nephew. "Okay, Shawn, one glass it is."

As they were all enjoying the heavy whipped-cream-and-macaroon dessert, the Rocking O ranch foreman arrived. "I heard a rumor that Bridey had fixed Irish Jig," he explained as he made his way to the last glass.

"You missed the glazed Irish tea cake, Rowdy," Jules told him with a twinkle in her eye.

He shook his head, his expression serious. "I'm betting Bridey saved me a piece," he said as a smile spread over his face. "I'll just take this on out to the barn. There's a heifer having some digestive trouble, and I don't want to be gone long."

Mac set his empty glass on the tray. "I'll be happy to give you hand, Mr. Thompson."

A scowl appeared on the older man's face. "I thought I told you it's Rowdy, not Mr. Thompson."

"That you did," Mac replied, "so in that case, I'll be happy to give you a hand, Rowdy."

"No need," Rowdy said before turning to leave. "I like my quiet time in the barn, and the old girl will be fine by morning. Beth Weston was out earlier and left a tonic."

Having met the young veterinarian only days after he'd arrived, Mac had found her to be quite knowledge-able about the stock, and he knew the heifer was in good hands with Rowdy. As Bridey returned to the house with the tray of empty glasses, he turned to his hosts. "How can you stand all that great food Bridey feeds you?"

Tanner sat on one of the comfortable lawn chairs, laughing. "I *am* spoiled. Bridey has been here on the

Rocking O since I was eight years old. I hardly remember a time she wasn't cooking up a storm."

When the others were seated, Jules turned to Nikki. "You're doing a wonderful job with the boys."

"Thank you," Nikki answered with a smile. "I'm enjoying getting to know them. They were hard to get settled down, after the arrival of the new horses and the barbecue tonight. It was so nice of you and Tanner to invite them."

Jules nodded. "We want them to know that we're like family here, both at the Bent Tree and the Rocking O."

"Knowing the boys aren't accustomed to riding, Dusty and I chose the tamest horses we could find," Tanner explained. "But riding is only a part of what they do here."

Nikki replied, but didn't look directly at him. "I've been making sure their schoolwork is done before riding lessons."

"I may be city bred," Jules said, "but I know from my own experiences that bonding with an animal, whether it's a horse, a dog, or whatever, is something everyone should experience, especially these boys. Once they can trust an animal, then they're more apt to trust humans."

"And themselves," Nikki added.

"Of course," Jules agreed with a knowing nod. "We want the Bent Tree to be a success. Not so much for us, but for the boys who come here. It may take some time for all of us to reach the goals we've set, but if we work together, we'll get there."

Tanner reached for his wife's hand and smiled at her. "Jules wants to help as many boys as she can. It's been a dream of hers for a long time, even before I met her."

"Which reminds me," Jules said, turning to Nikki, "there's a program I've heard about that you might find interesting and could benefit the boys. It's called Equine Assisted Psychotherapy."

"I've heard about it," Nikki said, nodding.

"It's only a suggestion," Jules continued, "but I have some literature you can look through, if you're interested."

Nikki nodded. "I'll be happy to."

"We'll talk about it more after you've had a chance to look it over," Jules said. "How did the riding lesson go this morning?"

Nikki smiled. "They can saddle a horse now."

"A wooden one, at least," Mac added.

"Wooden?" Tanner asked, looking at each of them.

Mac explained how Nikki had used a saddle frame and how well it had worked. He hesitated to admit Jules had made a good decision by hiring her. "She knows what she's doing."

"I never doubted it," Jules replied, smiling at Nikki. "Sometimes a person just knows when something is right. That's how I felt about Nikki when she applied for the job."

"Speaking of riding," Mac said, turning to Jules, "when are we going to take that long, lazy ride you promised me?"

Jules patted his hand. "In due time, Mac, when things settle down."

"That's what you always say."

Nikki looked at Jules. "I hate to break up the party, but I should be getting some sleep," she said, standing.

"I need to be turning in for the night, too," Mac agreed.

Nikki turned to Tanner. "Thank you for having us."

"Thank you both for joining us tonight. I enjoyed it," he told them. "Let's do it again soon."

Mac followed her around to the front of the house, wondering what had gotten into her, but after what had happened earlier, he wasn't going to ask. "Looks like Rowdy might have a long night ahead of him."

"Mmm."

Mac slowed his steps as they walked under the wooden arch and onto the Bent Tree grounds, and he let her go on ahead of him. But he nearly ran into her when she spun around to face him, her hands on her hips.

"Just tell me one thing," she whispered fiercely. "Is that what you call being comfortable with your employer?"

"What are you talking about?" he asked, confused by her sudden anger.

"All that dancing and touching and teasing."

He was speechless, unable to form a word to defend himself.

"Well? Is it?"

Gathering his wits, he chuckled.

"What's so funny?"

Noticing that her whisper was getting louder, he immediately sobered. "Nikki, Jules and I have known each other since we were kids. She and my younger sister competed on the same jumping circuit, and because our dads discovered they were fraternity brothers, Jules and I went to the same college. She's like a sister to me."

Nikki's eyes narrowed and she frowned as she looked at him. "Why didn't you tell me you knew her?"

She looked so cute when she was angry, the urge to touch her was almost unbearable, but he shrugged and stuck his hands into his pockets. "I never thought about it. Or maybe I thought she'd told you. It doesn't really matter, does it?"

For a moment she didn't answer, then she slowly shook her head and turned around. "It was just so…so weird, that's all."

It was an effort to keep from laughing, but Mac managed to remain quiet as he walked with her back to the main building. Sensing that anything he might say would probably be wrong, he didn't speak until they reached the doors to their apartments. "I'll see you tomorrow," he said without looking at her. But Nikki had already ducked inside her room and closed her door.

Stepping inside his own apartment, Mac collapsed onto his sofa. He could only imagine what Nikki had been thinking all evening. Was it possible she'd been feeling the tiniest bit jealous? He had to admit that if he'd been in her shoes, he would have.

CURIOUS ABOUT THE BOYS and thinking that being around them more might go a long way to helping him understand and know them better, Mac decided to join them for breakfast. He knocked on Nikki's door before leaving for the boys' dining area, but she didn't answer. Checking the kitchen, he didn't find her there and decided she must have gone ahead.

"Have you seen Nikki this morning?" he asked the boys when he discovered she wasn't with them.

"She was here earlier," Benito answered around a mouthful of biscuits and gravy.

Mac frowned at the boy's manners, but refrained from saying anything.

"She said she'd see us later," Billy added, and Mac wondered what had tempted her away from the boys.

A few seconds later Ray spoke. "Are we going to get to ride today?"

"We'll have to see," Mac answered. He knew the boys were eager, but he couldn't give the go-ahead without talking with Nikki first.

"But—"

"We'll see," he repeated more firmly.

Ray's mulish expression would have been comical if Mac hadn't been aware of how much the boys were looking forward to riding. With a glance at his watch, Mac took the last bite of his breakfast, finished his glass of juice and got to his feet. "Class time, boys," he announced. "Better hustle."

A collective groan went up from the group, but he ignored it. School hadn't been his favorite thing when he was their age, so he couldn't blame them, but he also knew the importance of an education. He hoped that when they got to be his age, they would appreciate what they'd learned and put it to good use.

When one of the teachers arrived to call the boys to class, Mac left the dining area and headed for the barn, hoping to find Nikki there. Maybe she'd heard something from Tanner about whether the boys would be allowed to ride later. But Nikki wasn't in the barn, either, or anywhere near it.

With a shrug of his shoulders, he filled the feed bins. The six new horses Tanner and Dusty had brought to the ranch were doing well. He didn't mind admitting that the two men knew their livestock, especially horses. But then, from what he knew about Tanner O'Brien, the man had been around ranching his entire life. Ranching and rodeo, according to Jules, had been Tanner's life, all while raising his nephew, Shawn.

Mac hoped to do a more thorough evaluation of the

new stock when Nikki was with him. She, too, had a way with the animals and seemed to know as much as Tanner did. His own experience was lifelong, from helping on his godfather's ranch in Idaho during summers to his and his sister's personal stock. He'd always enjoyed riding and was happy to be working where he could enjoy it, even though they'd not yet had the time to do that.

He was leaving the corral when he caught a glimpse of Nikki, heading for the main building from the direction of the boys' cabins. Even from a distance she looked tantalizing. Her long dark hair was loose, and her jeans molded her trim hips and long legs. As she drew closer, he noticed the top she was wearing. He frowned. What was she doing wearing a top like that around a bunch of teenage boys?

He was surprised to find her waiting just inside the building when he opened the door to walk inside. "Where were you this morning? You weren't at breakfast with the boys and—"

"I know I should have been, but… It's hard to explain." She stopped and shook her head. "I— Oh, never mind. I suppose I should tell you."

Exasperated, he simply waited for an explanation.

She drew in a deep breath. "It's… It's about Kirby."

"What about him?"

"I…" Another shake of her head before she tried again. "He—"

"Oh, for heaven's sake, Nikki, get on with it."

Her eyes widened, and then she nodded. "Last night after the boys were in bed, as I was coming from the office, I saw him."

She didn't seem inclined to continue, so he offered a verbal nudge. "And?"

"Well, it was dark in the hallway, and I wasn't sure

at first what I was seeing." She hesitated, but continued when he nodded, as if he understood, which he didn't. "He was coming out of the kitchen."

"Out of the kitchen?"

She nodded. "And he was dragging something behind him. Some kind of sack or a bag of some kind. I couldn't tell what it was."

"Did you ask him?"

She shook her head. "No, I didn't say a word. I was too surprised. He'd just gone out the main door when you came in and flipped on the lights."

"You haven't spoken to him about it?"

She shook her head again.

"What in the world would he be carting out of the kitchen?"

"Food."

"Food? But why?" he asked.

"I'm not sure, but I think it should be addressed."

He thought about it, trying to make some sense of it and failing. What kind of food would an eight-year-old boy steal? A boy who was given three meals a day and quite often a snack, too. "You're sure it was food?"

"I went to his room while the boys were at breakfast and found a pillowcase in his closet. It had food in it."

"What kind of food?"

"A box of crackers, a jar of peanut butter and two packages of cookies. None were open."

Considering the items stolen, it wasn't a big deal, but because some of the boys were at the ranch for reasons other than good behavior, he felt something needed to be done. "We can't let this go," he told her. "These boys are here because they have problems. He stole items that didn't belong to him."

"But why?" she cried. "They have plenty to eat here.

Why would he feel the need to steal food? I think that's what we need to focus on."

"He should be disciplined," Mac announced. When she shook her head, her lips a thin line, he knew he had a battle on his hands. Kirby was her favorite. "Look, Nikki, something needs to be done."

"We need to talk to him," she countered, "not punish him."

"I agree that someone should talk to him, but there must be some kind of repercussion for stealing. And that's what it was."

This time her hair flew when she shook her head. She just wasn't going to be reasonable, no matter what.

Sighing, he knew she had a point, but there needed to be more than talk. "He knows it's wrong, Nikki. You know that, I know that."

Her brown eyes flashed with anger. "Forget I mentioned it."

When she turned for her room, he reached for her. She spun around to look at him, and he noticed her anger had reached the boiling point. "Calm down, Nikki. Maybe we should—"

"I can handle it myself," she stated, pulling away from him and reaching for her door.

He raised his hands in surrender. "Fine. I'll leave it in your hands. You talk to him. And while you're at it, put some clothes on."

She stopped, her shoulders stiffening before she turned back to him. "Excuse me?"

"That top you're wearing," he said, pointing to the multicolored strapless knit thing that clung to her like a second skin. "Find something else to wear or cover it up. Teenage boys don't need that kind of encouragement." It was out of his mouth before he could stop it.

Eyes blazing with fury, she stepped closer and tilted her head up to look at him. "I don't believe you said that. I've worked with troubled boys, teenagers and younger, since I graduated from high school. No one has ever had a problem with my choice of clothing."

Angry at her for being so stubborn and even more at himself for saying what he had, he shrugged. "Then I guess I had to be the first, but somebody needed to say it."

Her eyes widened, and her mouth opened, but he didn't stay around to hear what she had to say. She was one stubborn female, he thought as he strode out the door and pulled in a deep breath. But he never should have said what he did.

Chapter Five

Nikki managed to avoid Mac for the rest of the day. She noticed he kept his distance from her, too, and she was relieved. Anger wasn't something she handled easily, and she didn't trust herself to be around others when it had taken hold of her. Even the next morning, forgiveness was not a part of her vocabulary, and she was thankful when he didn't show up at breakfast.

She kept watch and waited until she had an opportunity to find Kirby alone. Asking him about the food he'd taken wasn't the time to include everyone. Still seething over Mac's rudeness, she had no intention of asking for his help again. She certainly couldn't trust him. She would take care of it herself. His handling of the boys was too stern, and while they needed some of that, they also needed understanding and someone to guide them, not simply discipline.

"Kirby," she called when she saw him headed for the boys' cabins after morning classes. "Could you come help me in the barn?"

Even from a distance she could see Kirby's shy smile as he turned and walked her way. "What are we gonna do?" he asked when he caught up with her.

"Just straighten up a bit. It isn't hard work, but it'll go faster with two of us working."

He nodded and walked with her to the barn, but said nothing. Once they were inside, she pointed to a pile of saddle blankets she'd made sure were in disarray. "If you could fold and stack those on the shelf, I'll get the supplies we'll need in a few days when you boys will start riding."

His eyes grew wide with a look of wonder, and his smile, sometimes hidden, grew, too. "Really?"

"In a few days," she cautioned, "but we want to be ready, right?"

His head bobbed up and down, and he eagerly tackled the saddle blankets.

She waited only a few minutes, knowing Mac, who'd gone to help Tanner with Rocking O chores, could be back at any time. When she felt the time was right, she asked, "Kirby, why do you have a pillowcase with snacks in it in your closet?"

He didn't look up from his work, but she saw his body stiffen before he answered. "I do?"

"Yes," she said, watching and waiting.

Still without looking at her, he shrugged his small shoulders. "I don't know."

She'd expected him to deny it, but she also felt certain he understood that what he'd done was wrong. "Come sit by me."

He glanced at her as she settled on the bench beneath the tack, and he hesitated. Without a word he placed the folded saddle blanket he held on the shelf with the others and slowly moved to sit next to her. He didn't look at her, just sat silently, his head down.

"Would you like to tell me why you took the food from the kitchen in the administration building?"

His head came up and he looked at her.

"I saw you run out the door with the pillowcase behind you," she told him gently.

He looked away to stare at his shoes. "Oh."

"People take things for a reason," she continued. "If you'll tell me why, we can talk about it and see if something needs to be changed so you don't have to do it again."

He let out a soft sigh and began to speak, without looking at her. "When I still lived with him—my dad—there wasn't a lot to eat, so I found food so I wouldn't be hungry."

"Where did you find food?"

He shrugged again. "There are places." He turned to look at her. "Did you know restaurants throw away a whole lot of good food?"

She imagined him scrambling through a Dumpster, looking for something to eat, and had to suppress a shiver of horror. "Yes, they do."

He turned away. "And sometimes I stole from stores. An apple, a sandwich—not much, though. I didn't think they'd miss anything."

"Have you taken anything from the kitchen here before?"

At first he shook his head, but then he stopped. "Yeah."

"You don't need to do that, Kirby. We have plenty of food, don't we? Breakfast, lunch, supper and sometimes even a snack."

"I know."

"So you won't do it again, right?"

He nodded.

"And if you promise not to, I'll make sure that any time you need something extra, all you have to do is come tell me, and I'll give you a snack. Is that okay?"

Nodding again, he looked at her. There was a touch of humility in his eyes, but it was overshadowed by gratitude. "I promise I won't do it again."

Nikki smiled. As long as he knew he wouldn't have to go hungry, she was certain he wouldn't do it again. "Okay, then, let's finish this job and go find a snack."

His head tilted to the side as he looked at her. "Why?"

"Because I need one."

It wasn't long before they had everything tidied, and Kirby was on his way to his cabin to retrieve the pillowcase with the food to give to her. As she stepped out of the barn, Mac was waiting outside.

"You handled that well," he said when she stopped in the big doorway.

Still not ready to forgive him for the things he'd said to her the day before about her clothes, she shrugged. "As I told you, punishment and even discipline aren't always necessary."

Mac turned to watch Kirby running toward the cabins. "I don't know what could be worse than going hungry, but I guess it happens sometimes."

"It isn't uncommon for children to steal food when left on their own."

Mac shook his head. "He knew it was wrong, but he didn't like going hungry, and there was no one who could help him."

"That's what kids think. There are places they can go, but most don't know about them." Nikki remembered kids she'd met when she was growing up. She'd been lucky. Although she and her mom hadn't had it much better, there'd always been enough to get by. She'd never been left alone to fend for herself. But there were so many others who had no one. "We help those we can, but too many fall through the cracks."

"Jules said the same thing when I first came to the ranch. I never understood all it encompassed."

"The sad thing is, we can't help all of them."

She moved to step out of the barn, thinking of Kirby and all the others like him. There were so many who would never get the help they needed.

"About yesterday…" Mac began.

She froze. After all that he'd told her, why bring it up? "Don't worry about it," she answered.

"But I have worried," he said.

Her emotions were in turmoil, whirling inside her like a tornado. She didn't want to revisit this. Not now. But she knew it would be better to get it over with.

"I apologize," he said when she faced him. "It was completely uncalled for. I had no right to say those things to you."

She couldn't look at him. "It's done."

"It shouldn't have happened. Please accept my apology. I was upset. I was concerned for your safety."

She couldn't stop herself from staring at him. "My safety? In what way?"

"I know you don't see it," he said, "but dressing like that can be a temptation to the older boys." He smiled, but it was a wry smile and lopsided. "I know. I was that age once."

Her anger rose, but immediately vanished when she realized that he had been looking out for her. Maybe, just maybe, he had a heart under that sometimes stony exterior.

"I accept your apology," she said, knowing her own smile wobbled.

He offered his hand. "Friends, then?"

She put her hand in his, her smile feeling easier now. "Friends."

He continued to hold her hand for several moments. Of course it was innocent, she tried to tell herself, but the look in his eyes said more. So, unfortunately, did her heart.

MAC SETTLED AGAINST the corral fence and watched as Nikki wrapped up the day's riding lesson. He'd been amazed at how well they'd done, and chalked up her success to letting the boys get accustomed to their horses first. After that, each had taken a turn at dressing the horse, from brushing to saddling.

"Aren't we going to get on them?" Billy asked.

"Next time," Nikki answered. "You need to get to class, before I'm in trouble for keeping you too long."

A collective groan rose from the group, but each boy began removing the saddle from his horse. Thinking she might need a hand, Mac started to climb through the fence, but he stopped when he saw Tanner and his partner walking his way.

"I guess we missed it," Tanner said, disappointment in his voice as they reached the fence. "How'd they do?"

"Good," Mac answered before acknowledging Dusty. "I hope it was all right to let them have a try at saddling the new stock."

"You're in charge of that decision," Tanner reminded him. "You know more than I do about what she can do and what she can't." He looked out at the corral where Nikki was showing Leon how to fold the saddle blanket. "I'd say you made a good one. I don't think I've seen the boys this happy."

Mac laughed. "You missed all the grumbling when she told them they couldn't ride today."

Dusty stepped up to the fence next to Mac, grinning. "How do you manage to keep your mind on work?"

Mac had gotten to know Dusty well since he'd come to the ranch, and he returned the grin. "Do I need to remind you that you're a married man?"

"Very married, as a matter of fact. Happily, too," Dusty replied, his grin widening. "But I'm just saying…"

"He means well, Mac," Tanner said, laughing. "He did the same thing to me about Jules. We managed to turn the tables on him when it was his turn with Kate."

Before Mac could explain that his relationship with Nikki was business and nothing like what Dusty might be thinking, Nikki walked up to the fence. "Great horses, Tanner," she said, but her smile seemed nervous. "They were as nice as can be with the boys."

"I'm glad to hear it. I'm sorry we weren't here earlier. We've been trying to acquire a bull that Dusty's had his eye on for some time. We had the chance today, so we took it."

"And a damn fine bull he is," Dusty added, but turned to Nikki and touched the brim of his hat. "Excuse my language, ma'am."

"No problem. I've heard worse. Just be careful around the boys. By the way, I'm Nikki," she said, smiling, and stuck out her hand.

Dusty looked at it, then grinned at Mac as he took it. "Nice to meet you, Nikki. I'm Dusty McPherson. I'm glad the horses suit the boys. You sure have a way with them."

"The horses?" Tanner asked.

"Or the boys?" Mac finished.

"Both," Dusty answered, winking at Mac.

Mac chuckled and shook his head. If he hadn't known Dusty was harmless, he might have worried, but he'd seen the man with his wife, and Mac knew Dusty was not only a gentleman through and through, but he was head over heels in love with Kate.

As Tanner and Dusty talked to Nikki about her methods, he thought about how lucky both men were. What they had was what he someday hoped to have. But feeling unsure of himself and what he wanted to do with his life, now that he'd left the corporate world, he wasn't any nearer to settling down than he'd ever been. If he had been— He stopped the thought. Adding a relationship with anyone at this point would be wrong. Nikki struck him as someone who knew who she was and where she was going, while he continued to sort out his life.

"If Mac will give me a hand," Nikki said.

Mac looked at her and the others. "With what?"

Dusty elbowed him. "Pay attention to what the lady's saying."

Tanner explained. "We were talking about letting the boys ride again today."

"It would be better if you were there to help, Mac," Nikki added. "With both of us there, two can ride at a time."

Knowing how eager the boys were to ride, he didn't want to be the one to disappoint them. He might not understand them or be able to relate to them well, but he could understand how much they wanted to get on the horses, after spending so much time learning how.

"If you'll wait until later this afternoon," he said, "and if you can get the boys to wait that long, I can help you then."

"Great!" She turned to Tanner. "Thank you. I mean, well, the boys will thank you later, but—"

Laughing, he nodded. "Go on. Go tell them."

Nikki hesitated, but turned for the barn, where the boys were putting away the equipment.

"She really does have a special connection with the boys," Tanner said.

"She cares," Mac added, without meaning to.

"Like Jules," Tanner replied. He watched her enter the barn, his head tilted at an angle, as if he was studying something.

"What?" Mac asked.

Tanner shook his head. "I don't know. There's something…" He shrugged and turned away. "Come on up to the house. We'll see what Bridey's cooked up for lunch."

"I think I'll stick around and see how the boys react when she tells them," Mac said, hanging back.

"Good excuse," Dusty said, and chuckled as he followed Tanner.

Mac hoped his attraction to Nikki wasn't that obvious. But it was hard to ignore her. Besides, she deserved the praise. Chuckling to himself, he leaned against the fence to wait. He sure didn't want to hear how Dusty would twist that around.

Nikki appeared sooner than he expected. "Need some help?" he called to her as she headed toward him. She was only a few feet away when he realized something was wrong. Her dark eyes appeared larger than normal in a face that had paled. "What is it?" he asked, ready to vault the fence. "Are the boys all right?"

"They're fine," she said as she drew closer. "I just—" She shook her head as she reached him. "I have to leave."

"Leave?" he repeated as she climbed through the fence.

"I'll be back in a few hours," she answered. "Would

you watch the boys? I know I shouldn't be asking, but I have to—" She frowned as she straightened beside him. "It's a personal matter," she hurried to say, moving quickly away. "Could you let Jules know I had to leave?"

"Nikki, what—"

"A family emergency," she said. "Please, Mac." She was still facing him, but she was walking backward now. "I'll explain later."

He stared after her as she disappeared behind the row of trees, unsure what he should do. Tempted to go after her, he couldn't. She'd asked him to watch the boys.

The sound of her car starting and then the spin of tires in sand got him moving. Maybe the boys knew something. He'd do what he could until she returned, but he expected a reasonable explanation of what had sent her running off in the middle of the day, when she'd been so excited only minutes earlier about telling the boys they'd actually be getting on the horses later.

"Women," he muttered to himself. But deep down, he was worried.

NIKKI PULLED OFF the highway and into the gravel parking lot of the truck stop. Parking near the door of the small diner, she took a deep breath, got out of her car and walked inside the building. She glanced around the dingy interior until she found who she was looking for.

Sitting in a booth near the back of the diner, a middle-aged woman pulled off a pair of dark glasses and smiled. But the smile didn't reach her eyes. "You made good time," she said when Nikki slid onto the seat across the table from her.

"What's this about, Mom?" Nikki asked.

Sally Rains O'Brien Frederick frowned and replaced the dark glasses, but not before Nikki noticed how red her eyes were.

She's been crying. For a moment, Nikki felt bad, but then she thought about what Mac must have been thinking when she left without a real explanation.

"You're angry," Sally said.

"Damn right I am," Nikki answered, leaning forward.

Sally stiffened and sniffed. "Not half as angry as I am. What do you think you're doing at the Rocking O?"

"Who said I was at the O'Brien ranch?" Nikki asked, leaning back and crossing her arms in front of her.

Sally shook her head. "It doesn't matter. What does matter is that you went there, when I warned you years ago not to ever try to contact anyone there."

"It was Grandmother, wasn't it?"

Turning away, even though her glasses were dark enough to hide her eyes, Sally pressed her lips together before speaking. "Why didn't you tell me?"

Nikki had expected this. She'd been thirteen when her mother had revealed the secret she'd begged to hear all her life. They'd gone to Desperation, driving down the main street, her mother quiet beside her, never saying anything. Nikki had asked several times what they were doing, but Sally had only replied, "Just looking."

Afterward, they'd driven slowly by the ranch, and Nikki had wondered who lived in the big white house. Some time later, they'd stopped at this same diner. "That house was where I lived," Sally had said softly as they sat sipping soft drinks. "That's where my boys live. And your father." Her mother hadn't been aware then that Brody O'Brien had died.

There'd been no explanation of how or why, and Nikki closed her eyes, wishing the memory away. And all it had done was cause friction between her and her mother. She'd learned never to mention the trip or her brothers, but she'd sworn that someday she would return. And she had.

"I didn't tell you because I knew you'd try to keep me from going there," Nikki answered. Sighing, she leaned on the table. "Mom, look at me."

Sally turned her head and slowly removed the sunglasses, placing them on the table. "I warned you then, Nikki. I don't want your heart broken. They didn't want us. If they had…"

Reaching across the table, Nikki laid her hand on her mother's tightly clasped hands. "It's time to forget. It was a long time ago. You have a good life now. I have a good life."

Tears glistened in Sally's eyes, and she shook her head. "You could have had a better life. I should have thought of that. But I was a selfish young girl who only wanted to have fun."

"I've never blamed you, Mom. I understand."

"I wanted to get away from Tahlequah," Sally whispered, her head lowered. "And my parents. I thought marriage to Brody O'Brien would be fun, nothing more than riding the rodeo circuit together. But he wanted to settle down and start a family. He loved me, but…" She shook her head. "I couldn't stay, so I left."

"You left?" Nikki asked, her thoughts spinning. She'd thought Sally had been told to leave. "Did he send you away?"

Sally shook her head. "It was my decision. Raising two little boys was more than I'd bargained for, even with a man I thought I loved."

"But—"

"I didn't know I was pregnant again, not for several weeks after I'd left," Sally continued. "When I realized it, I quit riding and went home to Tahlequah to live with my mother." She raised her head and looked into Nikki's eyes. "After you were born, I realized how much I missed my boys. You were two when I had enough courage to call and ask to see them."

Nikki felt tears gathering in her own eyes and willed them away. This was the story she'd begged to hear. Shouldn't she be happier? But now she understood what all her mother's tears had been about for so many years. It was guilt.

Sally's smile was sad as she went on. "A woman answered. She told me the boys were fine, they didn't need me and not to call again or try to see them." Her eyes cleared and she smiled. "But I still had you."

"He didn't know about me?"

"I was afraid he might try to take you away from me if he knew, so I didn't say anything to the woman on the phone."

Stunned that none of her father's family even knew about her, Nikki also didn't want to upset her mother. That explained why no one had questioned her or seemed to notice a family resemblance. Now, after hearing the story, at least she knew why her mother had always been so protective of her.

"Why didn't you tell me these things before?" Nikki asked.

"I thought that the less you knew, the better off you would be. Maybe I was wrong to think that."

Nikki wasn't sure how to answer. She understood that her mother had been trying to protect her. She didn't agree, but it would be useless to tell her so now. Instead, she glanced around the diner until she spied the waitress. "Would you like something to drink, Mom?"

"I think I would, yes."

Nikki waved to indicate they were ready to order. "Tea or soda?" she asked her mother.

"Soda."

The waitress slowly made her way to the booth and stood holding her pad and pencil. "What can I get you, honey?" she asked around a piece of gum that popped when she spoke.

"Two sodas." Nikki tried not to stare at the woman's bright red hair, held back with a wide band that was decorated with a green polka-dot bow. On a young girl it might have looked cute, but on a woman of retirement age it was sad. "Lots of ice," she added as the woman wrote the order.

"I'll have it for you in just a few minutes, honey," she said, popping her gum again before she walked away.

While Sally shed her expensive linen jacket, Nikki surveyed the interior of the diner. It hadn't changed much in the fifteen years since Sally had brought her here after their drive-by visit to Desperation and the Rocking O. The walls were the same mossy-green they'd been then, but the color of the booths now matched, instead of the garish pink they'd been years before when Sally had revealed the secret to a stunned thirteen-year-old daughter.

"How's Roger?" Nikki asked, hoping to fill the silence that fell between her and her mother. She liked her stepfather, but when her mother had married him and announced they'd be moving to Louisiana, Nikki had asked to stay in Tahlequah with her grandmother. When her mother hadn't argued, Nikki had felt Sally cared more for Roger and was rejecting her for him.

Now that she was older, she understood it was her own insecurity.

"He stayed in Tahlequah," Sally answered, sounding more like herself. "Your grandmother enjoys his visits."

"She enjoys everyone's visits."

"You need to come back with me," Sally said, combing her fingers through her chin-length hair.

"I need to get back to work," Nikki replied.

Sally stared at her. "You're *working* there?"

Nikki nodded as the waitress returned with their drinks. "I'm working as a housemother to a group of young boys sent there by the court, and I'm teaching them how to ride."

For a moment her mother's eyes shone with pride, but she shook her head, as if what Nikki had said wasn't true. "They don't want you, Nikki, and I can't imagine how you managed to get a job there. Come back with me. You can have them ship your things."

Nikki had known that if her mother ever learned she was anywhere near the Rocking O, she'd do whatever it took to get her to leave. But Nikki wasn't going to leave. She'd finally found one of her brothers, and she intended to find the other.

"I'm happy at the Bent Tree Boys Ranch, Mom. Leaving isn't an option for me."

Sally pushed her glass aside and leaned forward, determination written on her face. "You'll only get hurt, Nikki."

"I'm willing to take that risk."

"But—"

"They don't *know.*"

Sitting up straight, Sally looked around the diner

before focusing again on Nikki. "You haven't told them who you are?"

Nikki shook her head. "I haven't decided yet if I will."

"But if you do—"

"That's my decision," Nikki said. She knew what she needed to say, but she waited several seconds for her mother to accept that she was now a grown woman, not a little girl who wanted to please her mother. "Did you think I wouldn't ever try to find them?" Nikki asked, keeping her voice low.

"I hoped," was all Sally said.

Even knowing it might be painful for her mother, Nikki had to tell her what she knew. "Tanner's a father now," she began. "His wife owns the boys' ranch, and she's a wonderful woman. I think you'd like her."

"I'm sure I would," Sally whispered, "if you like her."

"Their little boy is almost two years old, and he's adorable."

Sally hesitated for a moment, before she smiled. "So was Tanner. Tucker, too. Have you met him?"

Nikki had expected questions about the younger of her two brothers, but she still didn't have any answers. "No, I haven't. I don't know where he is, but his son is there at the ranch. Shawn is almost eighteen and lives with Tanner and Jules. I don't know him well, but I liked him the instant I met him."

Tears filled Sally's eyes, and she wiped them away with her fingers. "I always wondered what happened to them. I never forgot them." Her gaze met Nikki's. "If you tell them— Let them know I loved them, Nikki. Tell them I'm sorry. Will you do that?"

"Of course I will," Nikki promised.

Sally nodded. "I'll worry about you."

"I'll be fine, and I'll call you when I can. I'm sorry I didn't let you know, but…"

"No, I understand." She reached for Nikki's hand and held it tightly. "Just be careful. Don't let them hurt you. Please."

"I won't."

Hesitating, Sally nodded, then reached for her jacket. "Roger and I are going to Europe in the spring."

"How wonderful for the two of you." Nikki was glad her mother had found happiness and wished the best for her.

They talked about Sally's trip for a while, then decided it was time to say goodbye. In the parking lot, after promising she'd be careful, Nikki waved as her mother drove away.

Climbing into her car, she glanced at her watch. She had about an hour to come up with a reasonable explanation for leaving Mac to deal with her responsibilities. He wouldn't expect anything less.

Chapter Six

"But where did Nikki go?" Kirby asked Mac, a worried frown on his face.

Mac perched on the edge of Kirby's bed in the younger boys' cabin, hoping he could do this right. "I don't know, but she promised to be back later. And you know she wouldn't make a promise she wouldn't keep."

Kirby nodded, but he didn't seem to be cheered by the explanation. After dinner Mac had gathered all the boys together to let them know Nikki had needed to leave. Telling them right off that she'd be back, he decided, was the best thing to do. Other than that, he wasn't sure what to do with them. He wasn't accustomed to keeping boys of any age occupied.

"So what do you all want to do?" he asked. "How do you spend your evenings?"

Shamar shrugged. "Studying, sometimes. We could go watch television in the administration building."

"Or play Ping-Pong in the dining hall," Leon suggested.

"Can't we do something else?" asked Benito, looking bored.

"Like what?" Mac replied. He didn't have a clue. "Board games?"

"Nah," Benito replied. "Kirby always wants to play kid games."

"Right," Mac said, then shot an apologetic smile at Kirby.

"What did you do when you were a kid?" Ray asked.

Mac tried to think back to a time when he was their age. There were some years that he'd attended private school, but he wasn't eager to share those memories. He and some of the other boys at school had managed to get themselves in trouble, more often than not.

"I worked at my godfather's ranch in Idaho in the summer," he said without thinking as his memories skipped ahead.

"What was it like?" Billy asked. "Were there horses?"

Mac nodded, smiling at the memory. "Lots of horses. We rode the range nearly every day."

"Did he pay you?" Benito asked.

Laughing, Mac shook his head. "No, but the fun I had and all the things I learned made up for it."

"Nikki always makes it fun here," Kirby said quietly.

The other boys nodded in agreement.

"Hey!" Billy said. "Maybe we can do something special for her."

The other boys looked at each other. "But what?" Shamar asked.

Billy shrugged as the happy light in his eyes dimmed. "I don't know. It's just an idea."

"We could make her a card," Kirby whispered.

"A card?" Mac asked.

"Yeah," Benito said. "Like a thank-you card, maybe? For teaching us to ride."

"And we could all sign it," Ray added, bouncing on his knees on the bed across the room.

Mac wasn't sure whether he should tell the boy to stop, or if he should ignore it. He was at a total loss and wished Nikki hadn't put him in this situation. He could go up to the house and ask Jules to come deal with them, but he knew that wasn't fair. Nikki had entrusted the boys to him until she returned, and he'd told Jules he could handle it.

"What about some balloons?" Leon asked.

"Sounds good," Mac replied, glad someone had some ideas.

"The kind that float in the air," Ray added, still bouncing.

"Helium?" Mac asked. "I don't know…"

"I bet Jules has some," Shamar said.

"Why would she—" Mac began.

"Can we go ask her?" Ray interrupted. At least he'd quit bouncing.

Mac shrugged. "Well, I suppose we could try."

The boys started shouting, all of them wanting to go with him to the ranch house to ask Jules. Mac didn't think it would be a wise idea to truck them all up there, interrupting what he guessed was a quiet family evening for the O'Briens.

"Why don't I go ask?" he suggested. Frowns were his answer, but he wasn't going to give in. "Benito, you're the oldest. You're in charge," he said, rising from Kirby's bed. Turning to the others, he tried for his sternest look. "Nobody—and I mean nobody—leaves this cabin until I get back."

Resigned, the boys agreed, and Mac hoped he was doing the right thing.

Jules was pleased, as always, to see him at the house.

When he explained what the boys were planning, she was eager to help.

"We had balloons at Trish and Kate's baby shower, and I think we still have some helium left," she told him when he asked about the balloons. "Let me get Tanner to check. I think he locked up the tanks out in one of the buildings."

While waiting for Jules to return, he wandered into the kitchen, where he found Bridey. "Would you like a piece of cake, left over from supper?" she asked.

Even knowing he shouldn't, Mac couldn't resist. "If it isn't any trouble."

She fixed a plate with a large slice of cake and set it in front of him at the table, joining him there. "Jules mentioned that Nikki had gone somewhere. Is everything all right?" she asked.

Mac nodded. "As far as I know. She didn't say what it was about."

Bridey nodded, too. "Family, maybe. Has she ever mentioned her family?"

"Only a little," he replied, enjoying his cake. "Why?"

Bridey shrugged and stood, moving away from the table. "She reminds me of someone."

"Who?"

"Nobody you'd know," she answered, patting his shoulder.

Just as he finished his cake, Jules returned with a canister of helium. "Don't let the younger boys mess with this stuff, and for heaven's sake, don't let them inhale any of it!"

"What?" Mac asked with a grin. "No cartoon character voices?"

Jules shook her head, but smiled. "I know boys. Oh,

and here's a box with some balloons." She handed him two boxes. "The other has some ribbon. Maybe the boys can find a use for it. You can bring whatever you don't use—and the helium—back in the morning. Just make sure you lock it up in your room until you do."

"I will," he promised.

When he returned to the boys' cabin, he was greeted with whoops and cheers. After warning them that he'd be the one inflating the balloons, he saw Shamar turn to Benito with a disappointed frown. Benito's reply was a shrug, and it wasn't long before they joined in with the others.

Mac herded the boys into the common room in the main building, then quickly set to filling the balloons. Shamar had been voted in charge of making the card. Mac hadn't realized that the boy had so much artistic talent. There was so little he knew about them. If they hadn't been so busy and excited about the surprise for Nikki, he might have done something to rectify that. As it was, the whole experience struck him as controlled pandemonium. But he enjoyed it and so, it seemed, did the boys.

When the glare of headlights swept across the entrance doors and into the commons, Mac gathered the boys. Nikki was back. "Okay, boys, she just drove in. Why don't you take your places in the kitchen? Quickly, but don't make any noise."

The boys scattered immediately, whispering in excitement as they hid. Mac was relieved she was back. If it had been much later, he would have sent the boys to bed.

He'd been worried. She'd been so pale and in such a hurry when she'd left that he wasn't sure what to think. He only hoped it wasn't serious.

He heard the door near their apartments open and close, heard her footsteps, and then she called to him. "Mac? Are you down there?"

"Come on down. I'm in the middle of something."

Her footsteps echoed in the hallway as she walked his way. "What are you— Oh, my!" She turned to look at him. "Mac, what is this?"

She stopped next to the large round table, where the boys had anchored the bouquet of helium balloons, with a sign attached that read Nikki is the Best.

"There's a card," he said.

She turned back to him, her eyes brimming with tears. "Oh, Mac," she said. "Are the boys asleep?"

Suddenly the boys threw open the doors on the pass-through in the kitchen, shouting, "Surprise!"

In seconds they left the kitchen and swooped in on her, surrounding her. Laughing, she gave each one, even the older boys, a hug. They were all talking at once, a hundred miles an hour, but she had them calmed in a matter of minutes, asking questions. They beamed with pride, and Mac couldn't blame them. He was pretty proud of what they'd done, too.

After nearly thirty minutes she reminded them that it was late and sent them off to their rooms, with a promise to come later to tell them all good-night.

When they were all gone and the administration building was quiet again, he walked with her to her apartment. "Everything okay?" he asked.

She reached for the doorknob, hesitating, then nodded and turned to him. "I'm sorry I ran out like that. My mother called, and I was afraid something had happened to my grandmother. She's in her eighties and... Well, I worry."

Mac nodded. "She's okay, though? Your grandmother, I mean."

"She's fine. They both are." She stood at the door, watching him. "You put in a lot of work on that surprise. I can't tell you how much it means to me."

"Believe it or not, every bit of it was their idea. I only helped them get together some of the things they needed. We had a little help from Jules, too."

"I don't know how to thank you."

"Then don't." Uncomfortable with thanks he didn't think he deserved, he quickly changed the subject. "You're sure your grandmother is all right?" he asked.

"She's fine. I lived with her for several years after my mother married and moved out of state. My mother just…" She shook her head and sighed. "Families can sometimes be…"

"Yes, they can," he agreed.

"What's your family like?" she asked. "You said you have a sister. Any others?"

"Only Megan. She's two years younger than me. I was a horrible big brother."

Nikki laughed. "Somehow I doubt that."

"Ask Jules. I tortured both of them every chance I got."

"Your sister probably adores you, and Jules has obviously forgiven you for it," she pointed out.

"How about you?" he asked. "Brothers or sisters?"

She shook her head. "Just me and my mom. And grandmother." She turned the doorknob, then hesitated before turning back. "I—I never knew my father."

"Maybe that's not a bad thing."

She lifted her gaze to his. "Why?"

Shrugging, he looked away. He didn't know if he should share his past with her, but none of it was a secret, so it didn't really matter. "You might as well know that I came here to get away from my family."

Nikki's eyes were wide with surprise when he glanced at her. "Why?" she asked.

"I'd just learned that the man I thought was my father had adopted me after he married my mom."

Emotions scurried across her face. "But now you're here."

He felt her watching him and finally met her gaze. "It's complicated."

She sighed and leaned back against the door. "Life is complicated."

He couldn't agree with her more. Only Jules and Tanner knew the real reason he'd left Boston and come to the ranch. Maybe someday he'd feel more comfortable telling Nikki the whole story, but for now, he wasn't ready to do that.

"I've never been to a carnival."

Nikki looked down at the boy who held her hand tightly as they wove their way through the crowd of people attending Desperation's fall festival. "I don't think you'll be disappointed," she told him, pleased that she was the one introducing Kirby to one of the simple joys in life. She suspected he hadn't had many.

"Look at all those rides!" Ray shouted as they threaded their way through the amusement rides and carnival booths that filled the baseball field near the park.

"Is that a Ferris wheel?" Kirby asked, pointing to the tall, rotating wheel ahead of them.

"It sure is. Want to ride it?"

With wide eyes, Kirby nodded, obviously in awe of the tall structure spinning slowly, its baskets swinging gently against a clear blue sky. Looking around for Mac, Nikki finally spied him with the rest of the boys, standing several yards from a ticket booth. "There's Mac," she told him. "He must be getting tickets."

"Tickets?" Kirby asked, planting his feet and tugging at her hand as she tried to walk in Mac's direction. "We have to buy tickets?"

His awe and excitement had been replaced with disappointment. There was also a glimmer of fear in his eyes. "Why, yes," she answered, "but—"

"Now, don't you worry, young man," said a voice from behind her.

She turned to see a middle-aged man, a wide, friendly smile on his face and the same gimme cap on his head. "Mr. Barnes," she said, smiling. "It's good to see you again."

"Same here," he replied. "And it's Gerald to my friends. I consider you one of those. Tickets for the boys are all taken care of, if you'll just head on over to where Mac is. He's getting ride-all-day bracelets for all of you."

"All day?" Kirby asked. "Are we going to be here all day?"

Nikki nodded. "Most of the day, at least."

"Are we going to eat here, too?" Ray asked.

Laughing, Nikki looked at the two boys. "Can you smell all that good food? It won't be long until lunchtime. Why don't you both go join Mac and the others, and I'll be right along." When they were gone, she turned to Gerald Barnes. "Who's paying for these ride tickets?"

"Our local veterans group." He looked past her and grinned. "Seems there may be some trouble brewing over that, though."

She turned to look and saw two women about his age

marching toward them. The shorter of the two, her gray-ing hair laced with shots of red, appeared to be angry.

"Gerald Barnes, you know Hettie was planning to pay for the rides for those boys," the woman said.

"And I told you, we're taking care of that, Aggie," he answered matter-of-factly, "so it's a done deal."

Nikki was pleased to see that Mac and the six boys were walking toward them. She had a feeling there was a feud going on between the two women and Gerald, and she wasn't eager to be in the middle of it, at least without some allies.

"Tell the members thanks for us," Mac told Gerald when he joined them. When he glanced at the two women, Nikki was certain he didn't know them, either.

"Happy to do it," Gerald replied. "Aggie here isn't as pleased. Don't know how Hettie feels about it."

"Hettie isn't happy," the shorter woman said, a mulish expression on her face.

"It's all right, Aggie," said the tall, white-haired woman beside her.

Mac turned to look at the shorter one. "Aggie?"

"That's right," she said, looking him over from head to toe. "And who are you?"

"Aggie!" the other scolded, and then laughed. "You'll have to excuse our Aggie. She's a little put out with Gerald."

Aggie snorted. "As always."

The taller woman stretched out her hand to Mac. "Hettie Lambert."

"Nice to meet you," Mac said, taking her hand. "I'm Mac MacGregor, an old friend of Jules's. So this lovely woman with you is Dusty McPherson's—"

"Aunt-in-law, to be exact," Aggie finished for him. "Dusty is married to my niece, Kate."

Nikki watched with fascination as Mac released Hettie's hand and Aggie stepped up to offer hers. Mac took it and smiled at her. "I've had the pleasure of meeting your niece, Miss Clayborne, and it's a real pleasure to finally meet you."

"Dusty said you were a nice man." A smile lit Aggie's face and she turned to Hettie. "Mannerly, too, not like some people we know." She looked pointedly at Gerald.

"You haven't met Nikki, have you?" Mac asked the two ladies as he released Aggie's hand. "She's the boys' housemother and riding instructor."

Nikki smiled at them. "It's nice to meet you both." She could hear the boys behind her, starting to argue. "If you'll excuse me, I'll get the boys lined out." Turning to Gerald, she said, "I don't know how to thank you and the others for giving the boys the opportunity to enjoy the rides today."

"Giving the boys a chance to have fun is enough for us. Hope they have a great day."

With a smile and a wave at the others, she approached the boys. "What's all this noise?" she asked, looking from one to the other as Leon and Benito started shoving each other. "That's enough, you two."

"He said—"

"Doesn't matter," she told Leon, and flashed a warning glance at Benito. "Why don't you all decide what you want to ride and go have some fun?"

"Do we all have to ride the same thing together?" Shamar asked, glancing at Kirby.

Mac joined them and answered for her. "No, but stay in the area here with the rides. Don't be wandering off," he added, looking directly at each one. "It's almost eleven o'clock, so you need to meet us back here at noon."

"Only an hour?" Ray asked.

"You'll be ready for lunch by then," Mac answered. "I'm already thinking about food."

"I don't have a watch," Billy said.

"Just ask someone, or stay with one of the boys who has one," Nikki said. "Does everyone understand the rules?"

After they all nodded eagerly, they scattered in two different directions. The three younger boys went one way, while Benito, Shamar and Leon went another. Nikki and Mac wandered the grounds near the baseball field at the edge of town, where the carnival rides were set up. Seeing all the people who seemed to know each other well, she felt like a visitor in a strange world.

"This is a test for the boys, I guess," Mac said.

Shading her eyes with her hand, Nikki looked up at him. "A test?"

"As far as I know, they haven't been left on their own this much since the day they arrived at the ranch."

"I hadn't thought of that," she admitted. Her childhood had been much the same, always under the watchful eyes of her mother. Her grandmother had been more lenient, and Nikki had reveled in the time she spent with her.

"They'll do okay," Mac said, easing her mind a little. "There's plenty to keep them busy, at least until lunch."

The hour went quickly and they were soon rounding up the six boys. "Is anybody else ready for some food?" Nikki asked.

A chorus of different degrees of starving came from

the boys, but Nikki's attention was suddenly caught by someone else. "Is that Dusty waving to us?"

"Yeah, it is," Mac answered as Dusty walked toward him.

"You two look a little lost," Dusty said when he reached them. "Why don't you bring the boys over to Kate's booth? She made a ton of barbecued beef sandwiches, and there's all kinds of pie for dessert."

"Sounds good to me," Mac said, then turned to Nikki and the boys. "What do you all think?"

The boys agreed it was a great idea, and so did Nikki. Barbecued beef would be even better than the hot dogs she'd been thinking about, and she was eager to meet Dusty's wife.

Dusty took Nikki's hand, looping it through his arm, and led them to the park where various booths were set up.

"You know who he is?" Billy, following behind, asked the other boys in a loud whisper.

"Yeah, he's Tanner's partner," Shamar answered.

"He's a *bull rider*," Billy corrected.

"And Tanner's a world champion bronc rider," Benito pointed out. "So what?"

Dusty, who must have been listening, looked over his shoulder. "Bulls are bigger."

Nikki had to laugh. From what she'd seen and heard about Dusty, he had a heart of gold.

When they finally reached his wife's booth, Nikki was certain she could have sniffed her way to it. After introductions to Kate and her sister Trish, both of whom Nikki liked immediately, plates were filled with sandwiches and coleslaw, and soft drinks were passed out to the boys.

"Find a picnic table," Mac instructed, pointing to the

tables deeper in the park. "We'll join you in a few minutes." He dug into his pocket and turned to Kate. "How much do I owe you?"

"Nothing," Dusty said. "Put your money away. It's been taken care of."

"Taken care of?" Nikki asked.

Kate nodded. "Hettie came by earlier and plunked down the money and told Dusty to make sure you all came here to eat. She and Aunt Aggie were both a bit put out with Gerald Barnes," she added, laughing. "Hettie'd had her heart set on paying for the boys' rides."

Nikki could hardly believe it. "Everyone is so generous," she said. "I'll make sure the boys thank them."

"Hettie will like that," Kate said.

Hearing a disgusted snort, Nikki looked up.

"Tanner and Jules never should have opened that place and brought those boys here," a woman was saying. "No one will be safe in these parts."

"Letha, I don't think—" a timid-looking woman next to her said, glancing around.

"Don't shush me, Caroline. I have a right to say what I think," Letha replied.

Kate stepped forward. "Can I get you a sandwich, Letha? Or maybe some pie?"

Beside Nikki, Trish leaned close to whisper, "Don't mind her. Letha Atkins doesn't like anybody or anything."

Nikki simply smiled, recognizing the woman's voice from the Chick-a-Lick Café, but the woman's remark stung nonetheless. Obviously Desperation wasn't paradise after all.

Kate finished with the sale and turned around to place her hand on Nikki's arm. "There are lots of people in

Desperation who want to help make the Bent Tree a success. Don't let Letha make you think otherwise."

After they'd finished lunch, the boys were restless to join the fun again, and the rest of the day was spent playing games of chance in the park and taking a few more carnival rides. Nikki searched for the boys and found them in a group, admiring something Benito was holding.

"What's that?" she asked, expecting to see one of the prizes he'd won. Instead, he was holding a ten-dollar bill.

"There was this old lady," Benito said, and Nikki refrained from correcting his choice of words. "She was following some old guy, and she dropped something, but I guess she didn't know it. I picked it up and took it to her, and she gave me this." He held out the money to Nikki.

"It's yours, then," she told him.

"I can keep it?" he asked.

"It's a reward. You earned it."

When she told Mac the story after he joined them, he smiled. "Sounds like Vern and Esther."

"Who?" Nikki asked.

"An elderly couple I've seen around town. Rumor is that she's been chasing him for years, but he isn't getting caught."

Nikki looked at him, uncertain whether to believe the strange story or not. "Really?"

"Really. At least, that's what I've heard."

By the time the rides were beginning to shut down for the day, the stars were twinkling and the boys had their arms full of the prizes they'd won.

"Aren't you going to ride something?" Leon asked

Nikki as they made their way across the baseball field.

"That's okay," Nikki answered. "We're ready to go home. Aren't you all just a little tired?"

The boys claimed they weren't, but Nikki noticed they didn't have the energy they'd had that morning when they'd arrived. She suspected even Mac was feeling a little worn out.

"You can ride the Ferris wheel," Kirby said, taking her arm and tugging her in that direction. "And Mac can ride with you if you're scared."

She dared a glance at Mac, whose eyebrows were raised, but he was smiling slightly. There was no way to know what that meant, and she decided not to guess. It might seem natural to Kirby for her to ride with Mac, but her heart beat faster just thinking about it.

Shamar slung an arm across Kirby's shoulders. "Maybe Mac's the one who's scared," he said, shooting Mac a daring smile.

"Me scared?" Mac asked, winking at Kirby. "Not a bit. Come on, Nikki. Let's go show them how to ride a Ferris wheel the right way."

Taking an instinctive step back, Nikki wished the flutter in her stomach would stop—and it wasn't there because of the thought of riding a Ferris wheel. She hoped her nervous laugh didn't give her away, and said, "I'm afraid I don't know the right way. I guess you'll have to show them all by yourself."

He took her hand, surprising her, and led her in the direction of the Ferris wheel. "Then you admit you're afraid."

"No, of course not!"

"Better prove it, then."

A look at the boys was all she needed to know that

there was no way she was going to get out of this. Out-numbered, she let him lead her to the big wheel. And the flutters only got worse.

"See? It's not so bad, is it?" Mac asked while they were stopped at the top of the ride.

"I'm not afraid of Ferris wheels," Nikki insisted.

"Just of me, then, I guess."

Her head snapped around so fast to stare at him, the basket began to rock. Fear lit her eyes, and she reached for one of the steel girders that held the basket. "Can you help me stop this? I hate it when it rocks."

"Sure." He reached out on his side and steadied the basket. "Is that better?"

"Much," she answered without looking at him.

The wheel began its slow, circular descent, and he settled back in the seat, accidentally nudging her shoulder. "So you're not afraid of me?"

"Not in the least bit."

He wanted to tell her that maybe she should be. Denying his attraction to her had proved futile. He knew better than to get involved with someone, but it wasn't easy to ignore Nikki and the feelings he had for her, in spite of trying to disregard them.

"It's really pretty from up here," Nikki said, breaking in to his thoughts.

They were at the top of the wheel again, this time for the last time, and he'd made sure the basket didn't rock. Being next to her, nearly shoulder to shoulder, made him think of other things he would enjoy doing with her, and they weren't thoughts he should be having. He was grateful she wasn't a mind reader. If she had been, she might be jumping.

The wheel began to move again, and after two more

stops, it was their turn to step out onto the ramp. The boys were waiting for them, and Mac could see how worn out they were, especially Kirby and Ray.

"They'll sleep well tonight," Nikki whispered as they made their way to the Suburban parked near the ball field.

"I think we all will," Mac whispered back. "I can't remember a day since I was a kid that I've done so much. Work, yes, but recreation? Never."

"Only children have the stamina," she pointed out.

"So you're saying I'm old?"

She laughed, and even in the dark of the late evening, her eyes were lit with joy. "Only if you think so."

He looked at the boys, then back at her. "Compared to them, I suppose some would think so. How about you?"

She was quiet for a moment, and when she spoke, there was a wistful quality in her voice. "Sometimes I forget what it was like to be that young."

They reached their vehicle, and he unlocked the doors. "Everybody in," he said. For a group of six boys, they were quiet as they climbed inside.

Nikki was turned around in the front seat, making sure the boys were settled, when Mac slid in behind the steering wheel. "We're good to go," she told him.

He started the engine and followed the other cars leaving the makeshift parking lot. Quiet surrounded them as they rode to the ranch. A few glances in the rearview mirror assured Mac that the boys wouldn't give them any trouble about going to bed. From what he could tell, at least Kirby and Shamar were already asleep, if not one or two of the others.

When they reached the ranch, Mac drove across the grounds to get as close to the boys' quarters as possible.

"See if you can wake Shamar," he told Nikki. "I'll carry Kirby inside."

The boys grumbled a little at having to get out into the cool night air, but it didn't take long before they were all in bed. Mac and Nikki made sure there were no requests and all were asleep before they left them.

More than ready for sleep, Mac was awed by the blanket of stars above him. In Boston he'd hardly had the opportunity to see the night sky and had often wished he could. He was glad he'd made the decision to leave the city. The quiet of the country was peaceful. He'd missed it.

He was careful not to make a lot of noise as he entered the building and walked to his room. He'd just put his key in the lock when Nikki's door opened behind him. "I didn't wake you, did I?" he asked as she stood in her doorway, creating a tempting picture.

"No, actually I was waiting for you."

Surprised, the only thing he could say was "Really?"

"I wanted to thank you for a wonderful day."

"It was, wasn't it?"

She nodded. "Even the Ferris wheel." She opened the door wider. "I'm too keyed up right now to sleep. Would you like to come in?"

"Sure."

A small lamp near the door was the only light in the room, but he could see the artwork on her walls, and it fascinated him. "Did you do these?" he asked, walking closer to one of the paintings.

"My grandfather did. He was quite an artisan. Would you like to see more of his jewelry? Other than my ring, that is."

"I would," he answered.

She reached for a box and took out a silver bracelet.

When she held it out to him, he took it from her, fully intending to behave himself, but her fingers brushed his palm. It was her soft sigh that made him look at her instead of the bracelet at the same time she looked up at him, right into his eyes.

Without thinking, he touched her cheek, her skin soft and warm. He expected her to pull away, almost wished she would, but instead, she leaned closer.

"He died before I was born," she said, her voice as soft as her skin and her gaze locked with his. "I never knew him, but somehow I always felt close to him."

He had no answer to the sadness in her voice, and instinctively dipped his head, aware that she lifted hers. When their lips met, he knew he wouldn't be able to stop. In spite of all his denials, of all his warnings to himself, he'd taken a step he hadn't planned.

Just as he was ready to deepen the kiss, he heard a sound. Opening his eyes, he spied Kirby standing in the open doorway. Pulling away slightly from Nikki, he whispered, "Kirby."

She pulled back farther, her eyes dark and smoky. "What?"

"Kirby. He's gone," he answered, feeling a weight settle in his gut. They'd been caught by one of their charges doing something they shouldn't have been doing. Nothing could change that, but he hoped there'd be no damage—to their jobs, their relationship or to Kirby.

Chapter Seven

"Kirby was here?" Nikki felt a bit dazed by the kiss—a kiss that still vibrated through her. "Whatever for?"

Mac had stepped back and shook his head. He carefully handed her the bracelet, as if he was afraid he might touch her again. "I have no clue," he answered. "He was sound asleep when we left them."

"Something must have awakened him."

"A bad dream maybe?"

"I don't know." Nikki, avoiding thoughts of the kiss they'd shared, was shaken that Kirby might have seen them. There hadn't been a lot of time between getting the boys settled into bed and Mac's visit. "Maybe I should go check on him."

"Maybe you shouldn't."

"Why not?" she asked, looking up at him into his worried blue eyes.

"He may be embarrassed for walking in on two adults. If there's anything wrong, he'll either be back or one of the boys will come get you."

She was uneasy about letting Kirby go back to the bunkhouse without knowing why he'd come to her room. "After all they ate, he could have a stomachache."

Mac's mouth turned down in a frown, and furrows cut across his forehead. "I'll go check on him."

She shook her head. "It's my responsibility."

"And it's my fault."

"Your fault?" Was he going to apologize for kissing her? She wasn't sure she could handle that. No one had ever apologized to her for that, and she didn't want Mac to be the first.

"I'm the one who left the door open. I hadn't expected…"

Here it comes, she thought. *The apology.* "I hadn't, either. You don't need to—"

"Apologize?" he finished for her. "I do for leaving the door open and maybe for the bad timing, but not for kissing you."

Too worried about Kirby, she didn't want to think about what Mac meant. "I'm going to check on him."

As she hurried in the dark to the boys' cabins, her mind was busy replaying everything that had happened. Just where was this headed? Did he think she'd enticed him into her room only to get a kiss? *Had she?*

She tried shaking the strange thoughts from her head and had succeeded by the time she quietly opened the door to the cabin and tiptoed to Kirby's room. She found him in his bed, sound asleep.

Hurrying back to the main building in the chilly night air, she slipped into her room and closed the door with a sigh. She was positive she wouldn't get a wink of sleep.

WHEN MAC APPEARED to help her with the riding lesson the next morning, they decided to forget the whole thing and hope Kirby put it behind him, too.

The boys claimed their attention, ready to start the lesson, so there was no time left for discussion. After drawing straws to see who would go first, the boys mounted their horses, walking them around the corral in pairs, without problems. But Nikki felt different when around Mac, even though she knew it could all be for nothing. She couldn't get her hopes up that he had some kind of feeling for her. He didn't know her, at least, not everything.

Confusion was the word for the day. She wondered if she should tell Tanner she was his sister, but her mother's warning still echoed in her mind. There was always the possibility that he wouldn't want her to stay at the Bent Tree when he learned the truth, and she didn't know if she could handle the rejection, not to mention her mother's I-told-you-so.

By midweek, the kiss she'd shared with Mac was almost forgotten. Almost. Nikki had seen such an improvement with the boys' riding that she had an idea. She wanted to run her idea by Mac first before approaching Jules about it, but Tanner had borrowed him for the day.

"What an improvement!" Jules said when the morning lesson was over.

Nikki grinned, unable to hide how proud she was of the boys. She joined Jules at the fence and watched the boys as they dressed down their horses, taking the equipment into the barn. "We switched to two lessons a day, at least for now," she explained. "The boys are loving it."

Jules laughed as she watched them. "That's pretty obvious." As the last of them disappeared into the barn, she turned to Nikki. "Have you had a chance to look over the EAP information?"

Nikki felt a prick of guilt. Knowing she didn't have the money or the time, she hadn't been eager to learn more about something she could probably never do. "Not really," she said in all honesty. "The riding lessons have taken up most of my time." She took a few steps away before offering an apologetic smile. "And I'd better go make sure the boys are cleaning the tack right."

"When you have time," Jules called to her as she started for the barn.

"I will," Nikki called back. *Someday. Maybe.*

In the barn she watched the boys clean and check the equipment, giving encouragement and a few pointers on things they missed. They were nearly finished when she heard the sound of boot heels tapping concrete and saw that Mac had returned. The boys saw him, too, and called out greetings to him.

"I'm glad you're here," Nikki told him when the boys had finished and gone to wash up for lunch. "I have this idea I wanted to run by you."

He folded his arms and settled against the nearest stall. "Go ahead. I'm listening."

She smiled. "The boys have improved so much that I'd like to reward them."

"Another campfire?"

Now that she was sharing her idea, her enthusiasm grew. "No, I was thinking of some kind of riding exhibition where they could show off what they've learned."

"That's a great idea, and much better than a certificate or something like that." He looked down at her. "Good thinking, Nikki."

While she finished the last of the chores, she explained the different things she thought the boys could do. "I'll have to okay it with Jules, of course."

"Maybe there'll be time to do it this weekend."

They made plans to meet with Jules on Saturday, and then Mac headed for the dining area, while Nikki went to the sink at the back of the barn. When she was done, she reached for the turquoise ring her grandfather had made, but couldn't find it. She rarely wore it while riding, knowing there was a chance she might catch it on something, so she usually left it on the ledge over the barn sink. Searching more carefully, and lunch forgotten, she still couldn't find it. Her heart ached at the loss of it. She'd put up some signs and ask the boys if they'd seen it. Maybe someone had found it and would return it to her soon.

NIKKI COULD SMELL the dampness in the morning air before she opened her eyes. *Rain.* There hadn't been any in the two and a half weeks she'd been at the ranch. It was needed, but it definitely put a damper on her plans for the day.

Rolling out of bed, she realized she'd overslept. Although the weekends were technically her days off, she still spent most of her time with the boys. But today was the day they'd planned to talk to Jules about a reward for the boys.

She showered and dressed with haste, grabbing a jacket on the way to the door. Even inside, she could tell the weather had turned colder. When she stepped into the hallway, intending to check on the boys, Mac was just stepping inside the building.

"The boys are in the dining hall, playing board games with Shawn. No riding today," he said, wiping drops of rain from his face.

"Thanks." Nikki decided he looked as good wet as he did dry. Maybe even better.

"This might be a good time to talk to Jules about your idea for the boys," he suggested.

"I was thinking the same thing, but maybe it would be better to wait until the rain lets up a little."

"I have a fix for that." He ducked inside his apartment while she waited, and reappeared with an umbrella. "It's always a good idea to be prepared for a wet day," he told her as they stepped outside the building.

"It's rained today a lot more than I'd thought," she admitted as she huddled next to him under the umbrella and tried to keep up with his long stride.

Crossing the drive that separated the Bent Tree from the Rocking O, she stepped into a hole full of water and winced. At least she'd pulled on a pair of tennis shoes instead of her boots. They were almost to the house when Tanner's pickup pulled into the long drive and then up to the house.

"Good day for a duck," he greeted them when he got out of the truck.

Nikki looked up at the gray sky and wished to see it blue again. Her idea hinged on good weather and lots of practice. "Is it supposed to stop soon?"

Tanner nodded as he joined them on the walk that led to the house. "In a couple of hours it should start to clear up."

"My weatherman," Jules said from the doorway as she watched them, a warm smile on her face. "Have you all had breakfast?"

Nikki shook her head.

Jules held the door open for them as they stepped onto the porch. "Good. Bridey was just complaining that she'd made too much. Shawn had breakfast with the boys, so there's more here than we'll eat."

The rain and damp caused Nikki to shiver as she stepped inside the house, and she noticed how wet one foot was. "I should take off my shoes," she said. "I stepped in a puddle of water on the way. I don't want to track through your house."

"Oh, Nikki, you're shivering!" Jules helped her with her shoe, and then turned to her husband. "Tanner, take Mac on back while I help Nikki. And tell Bridey we have two more for breakfast."

"I'll be fine," Nikki assured her, her teeth beginning to chatter from the cold.

"But you aren't." Jules put a gentle hand on her shoulder. "Come with me. We'll get you changed into something warm."

"Really, I'm fine. I'll warm up soon. I don't want to be any trouble."

"You're no trouble," Jules insisted as she led Nikki up a curved staircase. They reached the top of the stairs and Nikki followed her through a set of double doors and into a large bedroom. "The bathroom is through there," Jules said, indicating a doorway. "I'll bring you something to change into."

Nikki went through the doorway and found the bathroom. After quickly drying her hair with a towel, she slipped out of her wet clothes and wrapped herself in another big towel. There was a soft knock at the door, and she opened it.

Carrying fleece pants and a top, Jules handed them to her. "They aren't haute couture, but they'll warm you up. Just hand me your wet clothes when you've finished dressing, and I'll put them in the dryer while we have breakfast. They'll be dry by the time we're finished, and maybe the rain will have stopped."

Nikki quickly changed and joined Jules in the large bedroom, complete with fireplace. White and gold dominated the room, from the huge four-poster bed to the drapes and carpet. "This is a beautiful room."

"I was going to redecorate after we married, but it

was so lovely, I couldn't," Jules told her as Nikki handed her the damp clothing.

Nikki wondered if it was the same as it had been when her mother had lived here, and couldn't imagine how her mother could leave such a place.

She followed Jules back down the stairs. "Feeling warm yet?" Jules asked. "The damp just seems to seep in, doesn't it?"

Nikki nodded. "I'm much better, thank you."

Jules's smile was comforting. "Do you drink coffee?" When Nikki answered that she did, Jules said, "Good, because I'm sure Bridey has a cup ready and waiting for you."

Jules led her to a charming nook just off the kitchen, where the others were seated at the table. Nikki felt a blush when the men, including Rowdy, stood when she and Jules entered the room. "There's a seat over there for you, Nikki."

Nikki took the seat next to Mac that Jules had indicated and carefully picked up the steaming mug of coffee in front of her. Just the steam from the drink warmed her, and she took a sip.

"Feeling better?" Tanner asked from across the table where he sat next to his wife.

Nikki set the cup down when she realized he was talking to her. "Much better, thank you." Feeling exposed with his attention on her, she placed her hands in her lap. Instead of twisting her ring as she usually did when she was nervous, she remembered she wasn't wearing it and quickly clasped her hands.

"Mac was telling me about an idea you had," he continued.

Nikki felt an instant of panic. She hadn't expected to be telling Tanner, only Jules. But neither was she ready to give up the opportunity to share her idea. She only hoped they'd find it acceptable.

Taking a deep breath, she tried for what she hoped was a confident smile. "The boys have done so well with their riding this week that I wanted to do something special for them," she explained. "I thought of several things. Certificates, a cake, maybe a trip somewhere." She stopped suddenly and looked at Tanner and Jules. "If you allowed it, of course."

Jules nodded and smiled, while Tanner asked, "And what did you come up with?"

Nikki returned the smile before answering him. "A way for them to show off their new skills."

Jules leaned forward. "How?"

"Something like a rodeo," Nikki answered, "where they could show off how they can saddle their horse, go through some of the exercises they've learned and just generally show that they can ride, after a lot of hard work."

"I like the idea," Tanner said, looking at his wife.

"We could invite some friends," Jules suggested. "Hettie would love to come. She's always asking how the boys are and what she can do to help."

"And Dusty, Kate—"

"Trish, Morgan, Aggie… Whoever wants to come," Jules finished. She turned to Nikki. "Would that be all right? Just a few friends. They've all been curious after meeting the boys at the fall festival."

Mac looked at Nikki. "Will that bother them? Having a bigger audience with people they hardly know, I mean."

Shaking her head, Nikki addressed Jules. "I think they'd love it. They're itching to show off their new skills."

"Typical boys," Jules said, laughing. "I think it's a wonderful idea. When were you thinking of doing this?"

"Next Saturday," Nikki answered.

"A week from today?" Tanner asked, glancing at Jules with a slight frown. "Are you sure they'll be ready?"

Mac answered before Nikki could. "They'll be ready."

Nikki nodded in agreement and gave Mac a warm smile, grateful for his support.

Bridey came in with a platter of scrambled eggs and another of sausage links, and Mac leaned closer to Nikki while everyone's attention was on the food. "I told you it was a good idea."

Nikki hoped it was. There was a lot of work to be done, and she prayed she was up to the task. It wouldn't be a good thing if she and the boys didn't pull this off.

MAC'S RADAR WAS UP. He'd noticed Nikki had been quiet for the past couple of days, but hadn't asked. One lesson learned.

They were checking the equipment in the tack room after the boys had finished their afternoon ride when he decided it was time to find out what was going on. "You're distracted," he told her.

She was sitting on a bench at the other side of the small room, and her hands stilled for a moment. "You're imagining things."

"No," he countered.

Sighing, she looked at him. "All right. I lost my turquoise ring."

"The one your grandfather made?"

"Yes. It was a graduation gift from my grandmother, and it means the world to me." Her eyes sparkled with unshed tears, but she didn't falter. "I always leave it on the ledge over the sink when I work with the horses. It wasn't there when I went to get it."

"You looked on the floor under the sink?"

She nodded. "Yes, all around, but the ring is gone. I even searched my room, in case I'd left it there."

"Do you think someone took it?"

"Stole it?" She shook her head when he nodded. "No, why would anyone do that? Maybe it fell off and was kicked or something. I don't know."

Putting aside the bridle he'd been checking, he studied her. He understood how much the gift meant to her. But there was very little he could do, except search the same area where she'd searched. "Did you ask the boys if they'd seen it?"

She nodded. "And I put up posters in the bunkhouses, but no one has found it yet."

When she fell silent, he attempted to change the subject to the boys' riding exhibition, but she didn't seem eager to discuss it, so he let it drop. With a little luck, he hoped they'd find the ring soon. He didn't like seeing her so sad.

He was checking the grounds the next day for needed repairs to do, when he spied Ray with Leon in the circle of trees south of the cabins, where they'd held their campfire. It wasn't unusual to see one of the older boys with a younger one, but there was something about the way they were huddled together that raised his suspicions there might be trouble afoot. Their backs were to him and as walked toward them, he strained to hear what they were saying.

"I know it's hers," Leon said. "I remember seeing it the first day she came, and then Billy mentioned there was something special about it. I don't remember what, but she always wears it, except when we're riding."

"Yeah, I think I've noticed it, too," Leon said. "And you're sure you saw him with it?"

"Definitely. Somebody needs to tell."

Mac was only a few yards from them when he spoke. "You can tell me."

Both boys jumped, and Ray let out a yelp. Guilt was written all over their faces when they turned to look at him, but they'd managed to hide it by the time Mac reached them.

"Tell you what?" Leon asked, his eyes wide with an innocence that Mac sensed was a ruse.

"Tell me who took what of whose," he answered, "although I'm pretty sure the 'whose' is Nikki." When neither of them spoke, and instead started watching their feet shuffling in the grass, he knew it was going to take all the patience he had to get them to talk. He was pretty sure the "who" was Kirby, Ray's roommate, and after what had happened on Sunday night after the carnival, it made sense. Or as much sense as a troubled eight-year-old could make.

"We don't know nothin'," Leon tried.

"We don't know *anything,*" Mac corrected, and Leon made a face. "But you do, and I'd really appreciate it if you'd tell me everything you know. I'd like to help."

The boys looked at each other, as if secretly communicating. "Well…" Leon said, and waited.

Beside him, Ray bit his lower lip, and then shrugged. "You won't get mad at us, will you?" he asked Mac.

"Why would I get mad at you?"

"Because we didn't come tell you or Nikki."

"No," Mac assured them, "but I won't be very happy if you don't tell me everything."

Silence stretched between the three of them, while Mac waited for them to do the right thing. He knew they would. Neither one was a bad boy, but in spite of everything, they still seemed to have a fear of authority.

"Kirby stole Nikki's ring," Ray finally said, without looking at Mac.

Leon stared at the ground.

"Do you know where he is?" he asked. The boys answered that they'd last seen him in his room. "Why don't you let me take care of this?" Mac suggested.

Leon looked at Ray, indecision written on his face. "I don't know…"

Mac had a feeling he knew what the boys were thinking. "Look, guys, I won't mention how I learned about the ring, and I won't mention any names."

Relief washed over their faces, and they even smiled. "Yeah, yeah," Ray said, nodding. "That's good."

"Let's keep this between us, though," Mac added.

The boys agreed, and he sent them on their way. He didn't have a clue how to approach this problem, but he would do whatever he could to make things right for everybody involved.

When he reached the boys' quarters, he found that Kirby's door was open, and he stepped inside. "Can I come in?" he asked.

Looking up from where he was sitting on his bed, Kirby nodded. "Did I do something wrong?"

Just like a kid, Mac thought. Always on the defensive when it came to grown-ups. "Mind if I sit down?" he asked with a smile, hoping to ease Kirby's fears.

Kirby shrugged his shoulders, but remained silent.

Settling at the foot of the bed, Mac remembered an incident at the boarding school when he was young and how the headmaster had handled that particular insurrection. "I need your help with a problem."

Deep brown eyes widened. "Me?"

Mac nodded. "It seems Nikki lost her ring. You know, that pretty blue one she wears?" When Kirby nodded again, he continued. "She lost it, and I was wondering if you might have found it."

His eyes grew larger. "Found it?"

"We think it fell off the ledge over the sink in the barn, where she'd left it."

"No."

"No? You didn't find it?"

Emotions warred on Kirby's face. Mac saw fear, shame and pride, and hoped the boy would do the right thing.

"I—" Kirby began, followed by a deep, heart-wrenching sigh. "I took it."

"Do you want to tell me why?"

"I was mad."

"Mad at Nikki?"

"She was— She was kissing you." Kirby stopped and sighed again. "I was mad because she liked you better than me."

It was exactly how Mac would have felt in the same situation. "Nikki loves you, Kirby. And, well, she and I are… We're friends. Sometimes grown-ups care for each other in a different way, that's all."

It was clear that Kirby understood how serious the matter was, and that was the most important thing. He knew he'd done wrong. "Would you like to return it to her?" Mac asked.

Slowly Kirby nodded his head.

It would break Nikki's heart to know Kirby had taken her ring, but he doubted there would be any harsh punishment. She hadn't wanted any at all when Kirby had stolen the food. Thanks to her, Mac now understood there were other ways to deal with transgressions.

He'd learned so much from her. When he'd first come to the ranch, he hadn't known how to connect with the boys and had been uncomfortable with them. But Nikki had shown him that what they needed most was love and guidance. After hearing Kirby's story about not having anything to eat, Mac had realized how rich his own life had been, not only because his family had never had that kind of hardship, but because of how much they all cared about one another. He was learning more from her than simply how to deal with boys. He was learning forgiveness. All he needed to learn now was how to forget the past and get on with his life, whatever he decided to make of it. If only he knew where to start.

Chapter Eight

The boys knew the main building was off-limits, except in an emergency. Mac considered this visit as one of those exceptions. Opening the door, he held it while Kirby entered the building, looking as if he was on his way to the gallows. His feet barely left the floor with each step, his shoulders slumped and his head was lowered. The nearer they got to Nikki's door, the more slowly he walked.

Poor kid, Mac thought. Kirby had a good heart—he just hadn't had the guidance most boys his age had experienced. Mac had skimmed his file, and he suspected that some information that should have been there had been left out. He didn't trust Kirby's father.

"I can stay out here, if you'd rather," he told the boy, who stood silent beside him. Kirby's face was so pale the scar on his cheek was even more visible than usual.

Kirby shook his head, but didn't look up at him, so Mac tapped on Nikki's door.

The sound of music coming from the apartment quieted, and then Nikki opened the door. "Gracious!" she said. "To what do I owe this honor?"

Mac glanced at Kirby and nodded, adding an encouraging smile. After a deep breath, the boy looked at Nikki. "We— I mean, I need to give you something."

Nikki's eyebrows went up. "Come on in, Kirby, and show me what you have for me."

She glanced at Mac as if he would explain, but Mac remained near the door and tried to keep his expression blank. When Kirby didn't move, he decided it was time to give the boy a nudge. "Kirby?"

Kirby looked up at him again, and Mac could almost feel his fear. He saw the boy's chest rise and fall with a deep breath.

Nikki was clearly puzzled. "Please, sit down," she told them and curled up in the corner of the sofa.

Mac took the chair and nodded to the other end of the sofa for Kirby. "It's okay," he told the boy.

Kirby nodded, although it wasn't without hesitation, and then took his seat, stiff and proper, his hands clasped in his lap. "I did something bad," he finally said.

"Oh, I can't believe that," Nikki replied with a look at Mac.

But Mac was staying out of it. Kirby needed to be the one to tell her, not him. "Go ahead, Kirby."

For a moment Mac thought the boy would remain silent, and he didn't know what to do about it. Nikki needed to know what had happened to her ring, and Kirby needed to tell her. But if he didn't say something soon…

Kirby moved to stick his hand into his pocket. When he withdrew it, he opened it and tentatively held it out to Nikki.

Her mouth flew open and she leaned toward him. "My ring!" She took the silver-and-turquoise circle from the boy's outstretched hand and slipped it onto her finger. "Where did you find it, Kirby?"

He shook his head and folded his hands in his lap again. "I didn't. I took it."

She stared at him, her lips parted as if she would say something, but nothing came out. Shaking her head, she sighed. "Why would you do that?" she asked softly.

His answer began with a beseeching glance at Mac, who encouraged him to continue with a nod. "When we came back from the fair the other night, I—" He glanced at Mac again. "I saw you and Mac."

Nodding, Nikki offered him a small smile, but it was clear she wasn't comfortable talking about it. "I know. Mac saw you in the doorway. But what does my ring have to do with that?"

"I—" Kirby ducked his head. "I thought you liked him better than me."

Nikki looked at Mac, a question in her eyes. Clearing his throat, he tried to answer her. "Kirby and I talked about it, and I told him that you loved him and things were different with grown-ups."

Her eyebrows rose for a split second, then she quickly turned to Kirby. "He's right, you know. I love you and all the boys."

Kirby nodded, and Mac noticed a slight smile quivering on his lips. "Sometimes I miss my mom," he said, his voice almost a whisper. "I guess I was afraid you'd go away, too."

"Your mom was sick, Kirby," Nikki told him. "She went to the hospital. Didn't you go see her?"

He shook his head. "No, he wouldn't let me."

Even from a distance, Mac could see the tears welling in Nikki's eyes. "But you're here now, and we all love you," Nikki finally said. "We're not going to go away."

"Things are different now," Mac told him.

Nodding, Kirby hung his head. "I was afraid."

Nikki moved closer and put her arm around the little boy. "When you're afraid, you should tell me. Or Mac," she added with a glance and smile at him. "Grown-ups do things children can't understand, but sometimes all it takes is an explanation. I'm not leaving. I love it here at the Bent Tree. Don't you?"

Kirby nodded again and touched the scar on his cheek. He continued to keep his head down, even as Nikki held him.

"Is something else bothering you?"

"No. And I'm sorry I took your ring."

Nikki smoothed her hand on his cheek. "I know you are. And I know you won't ever do anything like that again."

There was no question in her voice, as if she trusted he wouldn't. Mac hoped somehow he'd managed to get across to Kirby that he cared, too. But he still had a lot to learn.

Kirby looked up at her, and Mac saw her brush what he suspected was a tear from the boy's cheek. "That's quite a scar you have," she said, her voice quiet and easy.

"I fell out of bed and cut it on a toy on the floor."

Nikki looked at Mac, who shrugged in reply. Tilting her head to the side, she studied Kirby. "Is that what really happened?"

"Can I go now?" Kirby asked, moving out of Nikki's arms.

Nikki released him, looking as if her best friend had deserted her. "Sure."

Standing, Kirby faced her. "I won't ever take anything that belongs to somebody else again."

"I know you won't."

When he turned to look at Mac, his face revealed his re-solve. "I know you won't, too," Mac told him. He watched as Kirby walked to the door and let himself out.

Several moments after the door closed, Nikki turned to Mac. "I don't believe his story about cutting his face on a toy," she said, fury mixed with sadness in her eyes. "Kids will say whatever they've been told to say by a parent. I've seen it happen, many times."

"You think his dad hit him?" Mac asked.

"I think it's highly possible."

"What can we do?"

Nikki shook her head and sighed. "Nothing. As long as Kirby sticks to his story and no one saw it, nothing can be done. I've seen kids who have moved beyond the terror and told the truth, but…"

"I know," Mac answered. "I know." Wrapping her in his arms, he wished there was something he could do for Kirby.

The kiss came naturally, without much thought, and was meant only to comfort her. But when her hands moved up his chest and settled around his neck, comfort was the last thing on his mind. He wanted more, was ready for more, but this wasn't the time.

Gathering all the resistance he could muster, he ended the kiss and stepped back. The starting and stopping was going to kill him. And after glancing at Nikki, he suspected she felt the same. Moving to the door, he cleared his throat. "Maybe we should concentrate on the riding exhibition."

He didn't even wait for a response. He slipped out the door knowing he never should have touched her, but not knowing how he could stop.

BY MIDWEEK, the incident with her ring was forgotten as far as Nikki was concerned, and she was able to focus on the upcoming show.

"Nikki, have you met Sheriff Rule?"

Nikki looked up at the tall man who stood the merest inch shorter than Mac, who was standing beside him. "No, I haven't."

As Mac made the introductions, the sheriff took the hand she offered and touched the edge of his wide-brimmed hat with his other hand. "It's a pleasure," he said before releasing her. "My wife has mentioned you."

"Your wife?" Nikki asked. "Oh, I know! Trish. Yes, I met her at the fall festival. Her sister, too."

"Morgan stops by every week to talk with the boys and see how they're doing," Mac explained.

"I was at a law-enforcement conference the week after you arrived," the sheriff added, "so I missed meeting with the boys and welcoming you to the ranch. And the baby tends to take up a lot of our time."

"Krista, right?"

The sheriff nodded. "Born in July."

Nikki couldn't help but smile. His joy was evident in his voice. "Babies are special."

He agreed, but it was Mac who spoke next. "Morgan is quite impressed with the boys."

Morgan nodded. "Whether it's you or if they're just getting used to the ranch, they're like a completely different bunch of boys."

"I'd say it's Nikki," Mac said. "At least most of it."

Nikki tried not to let on how embarrassed she was. "They do seem to be adjusting well."

"I hear you're having some sort of riding show," Morgan said.

Nikki nodded. "An exhibition, so the boys can show off what they've learned."

"We're all planning to be here on Saturday to see it."

Nikki prayed the boys were ready, but she didn't want anyone to know how nervous she was about it. Now that the day was getting closer, she wondered if her idea would be as great as she'd thought it would be. "I hope it doesn't rain."

Morgan turned his head at the sound of a vehicle coming up the long drive. "Looks like OKDHS is here. Probably the monthly visit."

"I'm familiar with them," Nikki replied. The Oklahoma Department of Human Services had made the arrangements so she could live with her grandmother when her mother remarried and moved to Louisiana, and later she'd been involved with them while working for Cherokee Nation Youth Services.

She watched as the car stopped near the entrance of the boys' ranch, and a petite woman climbed out. Jules appeared from the house and met the woman, a wide smile on her face.

Mac shaded his eyes with his hand. "She's early." He glanced at Nikki, but only for a moment. "She was here just three weeks ago."

"Maybe her schedule changed," Morgan suggested as the two women walked under the ranch sign and approached them. "And I'd better get back to town. Whatever you do with the boys, Nikki, you're doing well. I'll see you all on Saturday."

Mac and Nikki said goodbye, but Nikki was watching the two women. Jules waved at them and spoke to the woman. At least they were smiling, Nikki thought, but as they walked closer, she noticed Jules's smile falter. She also realized she knew the woman.

A shaky smile barely covered Jules's worry when she and the woman joined them. "Cheryl, I'd like you to meet Nikki Johannson. She's been working with the boys for the past few weeks."

"Nikki and I know each other," Cheryl Bickham said with a smile at both of them. "We've worked together a few times. I'm glad to know you're here, Nikki. You understand how things are done, and there's something I need to talk with you about."

"Why don't we go up to the house?" Jules suggested. "The boys are in class, and we'll be more comfortable." She turned to Mac. "I'd like you to join us, too."

Nikki shivered in the late-morning sun and had no answer when Mac looked at her, one eyebrow raised. Something was going on and she was afraid she wouldn't like hearing it. The only way to know for sure and ease her fears was to go with them and hear what Cheryl had to tell them.

Once they were settled in the O'Brien living room, Jules made sure they were all comfortable. Bridey brought in a pitcher of lemonade, with a promise of more goodies when they finished with their meeting. Jules sat in one chair, while Cheryl took the other, and Nikki and Mac shared the plush sofa.

Silence filled the room and was finally broken when Cheryl cleared her throat, then looked directly at Nikki. "I've heard you've become quite fond of Kirby Miller."

Nikki wasn't sure what to answer, but decided the truth would be best. "I guess you could say we've formed a bond, perhaps because he's so young."

Cheryl nodded. "It may be. And being the youngest, he's probably needed more attention than some of the others. It's okay, Nikki. It shows your emotions run deep when it comes to the boys and your job. But I caution you not to get too close. You know how heartbreaking some of the cases can be."

Nikki nodded and offered what she hoped was a small smile. The weight that had felt like a ton of lead in her stomach grew even heavier. This was going to be about Kirby. Would she need to tell Cheryl about the ring?

She noticed how Cheryl glanced at Jules before speaking. "Kirby's father has requested visitation."

"You denied it, of course," Nikki blurted without thinking. She was certain they wouldn't let a man who'd allowed his son to roam the streets of the city, often searching for something to eat, have time with that son.

"Mr. Miller is apparently eager to see Kirby."

"He didn't seem to care enough to be a father to him," Nikki replied. "I also suspect he was the one who put that scar on Kirby's cheek." Nikki's voice rose with each word. She didn't care. She couldn't let this happen.

Cheryl didn't meet Nikki's gaze. "Mr. Miller told the caseworker repeatedly that it was an accident and that Kirby had fallen on a toy truck."

"Highly unlikely, from what I've seen of Kirby."

Cheryl reached out and took her hand. "We only have his word to go by. You know that. And Kirby didn't deny it."

"But—"

Leaning back in her seat, she released Nikki's hand and continued. "Mr. Miller was assured that over a period of time, his son might be returned to him permanently."

"No!"

"I'm afraid it's out of my hands."

"You can't send that boy back to a man who physically and emotionally abused him!"

Beside her on the sofa, Mac moved. "Nikki—"

Nikki ignored him as Cheryl shook her head. "Mr. Miller will have supervised visitation," she explained. "No overnights until the court agrees, and that only after we confirm that Kirby wouldn't be in any kind of danger. Nikki, you know how careful we are about being thorough. And it's all been agreed upon by the court. There's nothing I can do. I'm sorry. I truly am."

Because she'd worked within the system, Nikki did understand. Cheryl had no choice, only orders. Her job was to follow them. Questioning those orders wouldn't get Nikki anywhere.

"I'm sorry, too, that I reacted so badly," Nikki said.

"It's understandable." Cheryl's sympathy rang true.

Jules, who had remained silent, leaned forward. "I've seen the same thing happen many times, Nikki. I was a Juvenile Attorney and also worked with CASA in my spare time. I started the boys' ranch for those who slip through the cracks, but I can assure you through my own experience that many times things work out for the children. Parental counseling can help."

Knowing how much Jules cared for the boys, Nikki gave her a grateful smile before turning to Cheryl. "Do you know who the caseworker will be?"

"I haven't been given that information yet, but as soon as I do, I'll let you know."

"You're here to tell him, then?"

Cheryl nodded.

Nikki glanced at Mac, who'd said nothing, but she hoped he would support her with what she had in mind. "Would it be against regulations for me to tell him?"

Cheryl seemed to consider it, and then smiled at Nikki, her own features easing. "I'll fill you in on the details."

Mac watched as Nikki politely excused herself after talking with Cheryl, and he followed her outside, missing Bridey's lemon-drop cookies. Nikki, he'd decided, was worth missing a lot of things for. Too bad he didn't know what to do about it.

"Nikki, I'm sorry. If I could—"

She was in his arms, her cheek pressed against his chest. "I can't believe this, Mac. I just can't."

"I can't, either," he told her, dismissing the fact that anyone and everyone on the ranch might see them. "And I don't see that there's anything we can do about it, except be there for him if he should need us."

She looked up, the sadness in her eyes making his heart ache. "I knew you'd understand."

He did, but not in a way she might ever know. How had he been lucky enough to have been adopted by a man who had raised him as if he was his own? He'd been angry when he'd learned the truth, angry enough to leave his father's business, where he would soon have been appointed vice president of the company—something he'd worked toward since the first day his father had taken him to work when he was little more than Kirby's age. He was still dealing with the anger that for thirty-one years his parents had hidden the truth.

Nikki sniffed, a sure sign that she'd been crying, along with a lone tear that now trickled down her cheek. "It's not right. He shouldn't be sent back to a man who hurt him."

"I know." There was little else Mac could say. The court had the final word. At least it was short-term. "They'll be supervised," he reminded her. "And it isn't like Kirby is going back permanently. It's a trial for all concerned."

"Do you think he told anyone the truth about how he got the scar on his cheek?" she asked.

"I doubt it. Or if he did, his dad insisted it was an accident." But, like Nikki, Mac hadn't bought Kirby's explanation.

Nikki stepped back, out of his arms. Looking around, she made a funny face. "I hope no one witnessed my little meltdown," she said, her voice wobbling. "I guess I should get back to…something."

"We both should." But he hated to leave her when she was distressed.

He walked with her to the main building, and neither of them spoke as they passed inside. All he could hope for was that Kirby wouldn't be upset when he learned about the visit.

Before they even made it to their respective doors, he stopped her. "You can say no," he began, "but if you'd like me to be with you when you tell him, I will."

Her watery smile nearly broke his heart. "I'd feel so much better if you were."

He reached out and touched her cheek with his finger. "You'll do fine. You always do. When do you plan to do it?"

"I told Cheryl I'd wait about an hour after lunch was over. I don't want him to miss a meal, and I want to make sure that meal is settled." Her smile was forced and lopsided. "Emotions on a full stomach can be dangerous."

She surprised him when she placed her hand on his arm. He was even more surprised when she rose on her toes and kissed his cheek, then disappeared into her apartment, leaving him staring at her closed door.

A kiss on the cheek? What did that mean? Probably

nothing to get excited about, so he might as well forget it. Not that he would.

He returned to his rooms close to an hour after the boys finished lunch and waited. When he realized he was checking his watch every two minutes, he pulled a book from his small bookshelf, settled onto the more comfortable of his chairs and tried to read. But his concern about what would soon be taking place made reading impossible.

A light knock on his door brought him quickly to his feet, and he hurried to let Nikki and Kirby inside. One look at Nikki, and he guessed this might be one of the hardest things she'd ever done.

They sat together on the sofa, with Kirby between them. "Did I do something bad again?" he asked, looking from one to the other.

Nikki slipped her arm around him. "No, you haven't done anything wrong. But we need to talk to you. Mac and I."

Kirby looked at Mac. "What about?"

Mac had to swallow the apprehension he felt before he tried to smile. There was no knowing how Kirby would react, and Mac suspected it might not be good. The boy was very attached to Nikki, and to everyone at the Bent Tree. "We had some news today from OKDHS."

Nikki glanced at him and hurried on. "Cheryl Bickham, the caseworker for the ranch, came to visit today."

Kirby swung around to look at Nikki. "I know her. She's the one who helped get me here."

"Yes," Nikki answered, a little too brightly.

She began asking him what he remembered about the caseworker, and Mac sensed she was stalling. And then he realized that she was setting the stage to tell him the news. He watched Kirby closely, looking for signs that he knew something bad was coming, but although the boy was a bit reserved, he didn't seem to suspect bad news.

"But why was she here?" Kirby asked.

When Nikki looked at Mac, he could see her distress. It was time for him to step in. "It's about your dad," Mac told him as gently as he could.

It was as if Kirby had flipped an internal switch. His features went blank, and he sat a little straighter between them, looking straight ahead. "What about him?"

Nikki glanced quickly at Mac before she answered. "He's asked that you come home for a short visit."

Kirby nodded slowly before he lowered his head. "Then I won't be living here anymore."

Nikki's head snapped up. "Yes, you will! It's only for a day, and there'll be someone there with you at all times."

"When do I have to leave?" Kirby asked, his voice flat and without emotion.

"Almost two weeks," Nikki answered, and rubbed his arm with her hand as she held him closer.

But Kirby remained stiff and as still as a stone. "Then I'll get to do the riding show."

"Yes, you will! Isn't that great?"

Kirby nodded again. "Okay." After a heartbeat, he asked, "Can I go now?"

"I…" Nikki began, but looked at Mac over the boy's head.

"It'll be okay," Mac told Kirby. "He'll pick you up on a Saturday morning and bring you back that night. You won't be staying overnight." *Not yet.* "It won't be like it was." When Kirby answered only with a slight dip of his head, Mac continued. "And we'll make sure everything goes okay, that he doesn't—" He had to stop before he said the wrong thing. "The caseworker who will be with you will make sure there's plenty to eat and everything goes okay."

Nikki quickly intervened. "And we'll be waiting for you here at the ranch when you get back that evening."

Kirby struggled to stand, and Nikki released him with obvious reluctance. "I want to go to my room now," he said.

Mac wasn't sure what to do or say. Nikki was concerned, and he didn't blame her. Kirby wasn't at all excited about the visit. In fact, Mac suspected there might be a little fear involved. But only Kirby knew what he was returning to, if only for a day.

Nikki followed Kirby to the door and spoke so softly to him that Mac didn't hear what she was saying. When Kirby was gone, she leaned her forehead against the closed door, bringing Mac to his feet. "He'll be all right," Mac told her as he went to her.

"I hope so," she said, turning to him. "But it isn't this visit that worries me. It's the future. Kirby's future."

When she stepped closer, he put his arms around her and held her close.

She took a deep, shattering breath. "I love him, Mac," she said, leaning back to look up at him as he held her. "Almost as if he was my own. We can't let anything happen to him."

"I know," he answered, stroking her long hair, "and we'll make sure he's okay." *Somehow.*

He didn't know how long he held her as she quietly cried in his arms.

Chapter Nine

"We've certainly been blessed with a beautiful day," Jules commented at breakfast with the boys. "I was so afraid it might rain, and we'd have to cancel the riding show today, but there's not a cloud in the sky this morning. It's like Indian summer."

Nikki nodded as she watched Kirby. She hadn't seen a smile on his face since they'd told him he'd be spending a day with his father, even though she'd tried to coax one out of him. Worry had disturbed her sleep, and she had to stifle a yawn as Billy handed her the syrup for her pancakes.

"What time did you say the new boys will be here?" Mac asked Jules.

She glanced at her watch. "In about half an hour. I was hoping Tanner would be here, but he won't get back until just before the show starts." She sighed and picked up her fork. "He's as unhappy about having to leave last night as I am, but at least the stock he and Dusty went to buy aren't out of state."

Nikki's ears had picked up at the mention of Tanner. She almost hoped he wouldn't make it back until after the exhibition. Her nerves were on edge as it was. Oh, she knew the boys would do fine. There was no doubt in her mind that they were eager and ready to show off their new riding skills. But she had a surprise planned for them, and for a short time the spotlight would be on her.

Nikki studied the faces of the boys seated down the table from her for clues of nervousness. "Don't forget to be at the barn immediately after lunch to get ready today," she told them.

"I'm not sure I'll be able to eat lunch," Ray said with a nervous smile.

"No kidding," Shamar agreed. "But who needs lunch? These are the best pancakes I've ever had."

Mac laughed. "You'd think this was the first time you've had them."

"Sandwiches for lunch," Nikki said. "There won't be a lot of time between lunch and getting on the horses. I don't want any of you getting sick."

"Oh, we won't do that," Shamar said.

But as wired as the boys already were, she didn't want to take a risk. "Just take it easy," she cautioned. But she added a smile. She was as excited for them as they were, and it was hard not to be proud of each of them. They'd worked hard and learned a lot in the few weeks she'd had with them.

Kirby looked up from his plate. "Are you going to have lunch with us?"

"I'll be here," she promised. "But like Ray, I'm not sure I'll be eating much." A chorus of "You can't be scared" rose from the boys, and she assured them she wasn't. "I have complete faith that all of you will be wonderful this afternoon."

They assured her they would try, even Kirby, with his somber eyes. At least if he was ever returned to live with his father permanently, he would always have the memory of showing off his riding.

The thought brought tears to her eyes. Because she didn't want anyone to notice, she put her napkin on the table and stood. "I think I'll go take one more look at the horses. I'll see you all at lunch."

"Nikki?" Mac asked, eyeing her with concern.

She couldn't hide her feelings much longer, but she managed a smile for him and the others, then started for the barn. It wasn't the horses she wanted to check on—she needed to get a check on her emotions. Seeing her sad or worried would only make it harder for Kirby. It wouldn't help the others, either.

Once inside the barn, where sunlight streamed in the windows, she sank onto a bale of hay, pressed her hands to her face and took a deep breath. "Just let everything go all right with the show today," she whispered.

A horse whinnied, and she looked up to see one of the large doors opening. It was Mac, probably coming to see if she was all right.

"You okay?" he asked as he came down the center walkway toward her.

"I'm fine." Pushing to her feet, she concentrated on brushing off the loose hay and dust from her jeans.

"You don't look fine," he said when he reached her.

She glanced up to see him studying her. "All right, I'm not fine, but I'm okay. Is that better?"

His hand came up slowly, and he touched a strand of the hair she'd been too rushed to braid that morning. "You don't have to be tough around me."

Still unable to look at him, she nodded. She was beginning to rely on him for strength, and that wasn't good. She knew so little about him, and he knew next to nothing about her. She'd made sure of that.

His head went up and he dropped the strand of hair he held. "Sounds like a car driving up."

Nikki listened more closely. "The new boys," she said on a sigh.

"Are you up to this?"

It took an effort, but she managed a real smile. "Yes." She had to be up to it. Kirby wasn't the only boy who needed her. They all did. They needed her, Mac, Jules, all of them. For however long, they were the family some of the boys had never really had.

She'd also decided she would tell Tanner who she was. Now that she'd gotten to know him, she felt it was the right thing to do. She just didn't know when she would do it.

"Let's go meet the boys," she told Mac, feeling more eager.

They were met outside the barn by Cheryl Bickham, Jules and the two boys. Jules introduced everyone, and Nikki was immediately taken with both boys. Twelve-year-old Jacob, with his dark, serious eyes behind wire-rimmed glasses, tugged at her heart. Andrew, a carrot-topped eleven-year-old, was visibly nervous, his freckled face reddening when she greeted them.

"I'm going to show them to the bunkhouses," Jules explained after they'd chatted for a few minutes.

"She loves having more boys here," Cheryl said as Jules led the boys away. She turned to Nikki and asked, "How's Kirby doing?"

"I'm not sure," Nikki admitted. "He hasn't talked about it. I haven't seen a tear, but I haven't seen a smile, either. To be honest, I'm worried."

"That's the way he was when I first met him," Cheryl said. "I think it's his way of shutting off emotions he doesn't know how to deal with." She laid her hand on Nikki's shoulder. "He'll be okay. We'll be keeping an eye on things."

Nikki didn't doubt OKDHS would do everything they could, but she also knew from personal experience that things happened that OKDHS never knew about, unless someone told them. She suspected there were several things Kirby hadn't revealed about his family life. All she could do was hope this first visit went smoothly. Her main concern now was to make sure Kirby was safe.

Needing to change the subject, Nikki asked, "Will you be here for the riding exhibition this afternoon?"

"I wish I could," Cheryl answered, "but I have family obligations today. I'm sure it will be wonderful for the boys."

"They're definitely excited about it," Mac said. "I'm not sure who's more excited, the boys, us or the friends of the O'Briens who are coming to watch."

"Jules has done such a wonderful job here," Cheryl agreed. "I wish we could send more boys, but the state tends to move slowly with these things."

As far as Nikki was concerned, nothing was perfect, but the Bent Tree Boys Ranch was the next thing to it. Maybe someday the state would realize it. She'd never been happier, and she suspected the boys had never been, either.

"I'd better get on the road," Cheryl announced. "I still haven't heard who'll be supervising Kirby's visit, Nikki, but I'll let you know when I do."

"Thanks, Cheryl," Nikki said. When she was gone, Nikki turned to Mac. "Maybe I should go check the horses again."

He shook his head. "I'll check on them. If you trust me to do it right," he added with a comical frown. "Take the rest of the morning off. Put on some music, read, relax, whatever it takes to get rid of some of those doubts you're having."

Nikki had to laugh. He knew exactly how jumpy she was feeling. "I trust you. And thanks."

"They'll do great."

She knew they would, but knowing it didn't settle her nerves.

MAC LOOKED AT HIS WATCH. What was keeping Nikki? It was getting close to one o'clock, and people from around Desperation were already arriving, but he hadn't seen Nikki since their quick lunch, when she'd wished the boys good luck.

"We'll have to build bleachers if we continue to do this," Jules, beside him, said with a laugh.

Although he knew he probably shouldn't be, Mac was surprised at the number of people who had come to watch the exhibition. "Looks like we're going to have quite a crowd."

"They're ready, aren't they?" she asked. "The boys, I mean. I know Nikki has faith in them and says they are, but…"

"They're ready. She's kept the whole thing simple. I think you'll enjoy it."

"Oh, I know I will," she said. "I guess I'm feeling the same nerves the boys must be. Nikki, too. And shouldn't she be here by now?"

Mac looked around the area near the corral, feeling the same nervousness Jules was, until he spied Nikki. "There she is," he said, pointing to the other side of the corral.

They watched as she spoke with some of the guests, all friends and neighbors. Mac quickly chided himself for being worried. Nikki wasn't the type to let the boys or the O'Briens down. Even as upset as she'd been about

Kirby, there wasn't a hint of it now as she helped find chairs and greeted everyone.

"I should go give her hand," Jules said. "She'll lose track of time if one of them starts bending her ear."

Mac laughed, agreeing, and started for the barn, where he found the boys talking in loud whispers. "Are you all ready?" he asked, and noticed that several of them jumped at the sound of his voice.

"Where's Nikki?" Ray asked.

"She'll be here in a minute," he assured them all. "Is anybody nervous?"

Five heads shook, while one remained still. Kirby appeared to have emotionally detached himself from the others, although he stood in the midst of them. Mac knew he needed to bring him out of it, at least until the exhibition was over. "Ready to put on a show, Kirby?"

For a moment the boy remained still, his eyes wide. "Yes," he finally answered.

Mac nodded. "Good."

Nikki walked into the barn, her steps brisk and self-assured as she approached them. "Five more minutes."

Mac looked around at the smiling yet nervous faces of the six boys. "They're ready to put on a show," he said, smiling at each of them.

"Just so you all know," she said when she reached them, "there's quite a crowd out there. Don't let it bother you. Everyone out there is cheering for you, so everything you do will be special to them. Jules will welcome our guests. After that, Mac is going to make the opening introductions, and you'll know what's next when he announces it. Any questions?" Six boys shook their heads. "Okay, then. I'll be close by, so if you have a problem, don't worry. I'll be there to help."

The horses waited, tied along the fence on one side

of the corral, when the group stepped out of the barn and into the bright sunshine. The crowd quieted. Each boy walked to his own horse, while Jules welcomed the friends and neighbors who'd come to see the show. When she was done, Mac took the cordless microphone from her.

"It's great that all of you have come out here to the Bent Tree Boys Ranch to meet our boys and see what they've learned," he told the crowd. He went on to explain how hard the boys had worked on their riding skills and how far they'd come since the first day Nikki had introduced them to the wooden horse. The crowd enjoyed the story, eager to see for themselves what the boys could do.

The boys began by saddling their horses. Mac, with Shawn's help, had built a set of steps for Kirby, and Shamar helped lift the saddle when the time came. The crowd loved it.

The show continued with the boys taking their horses from simple walking to trotting and loping. They formed two teams and rode a relay race along the length of the corral, passing off bandannas to the next rider. The exhibition ended with pole bending, as the boys formed a line and loped their horses in an intricate pattern around the six poles Mac and Shawn had placed in the ground.

The boys beamed with pride when they dismounted, and the crowd cheered them. Even Kirby smiled, Mac noted.

But to everyone's surprise, and especially to Mac's, the show wasn't quite over. Nikki appeared at the opening of the barn, dressed in Native American attire, her hair twisted into two braids and wrapped with rawhide and feathers. The horse beneath her danced, as if impatient to get moving. With a loud yell, she urged her mount forward, and the crowd watched, enthralled, as she raced around the poles in a fine exhibition of pole bending.

Tanner, who'd arrived right after Jules's welcome to the guests and now stood with her and Mac, suddenly turned toward the house and walked away. Jules caught up with him, and Mac heard bits and pieces of what they were saying.

"...leave now," Jules said.

"I can't watch it," Tanner answered.

"Nikki worked hard on all of this," Jules pointed out. "You can't just leave."

"I'll be back." He breathed out a heavy sigh. "It reminds me too much of Sally. I remember watching her practice in that same corral. It's just too much."

"Tanner," Jules called as the crowd whistled and applauded at the end of Nikki's ride.

Mac turned to look, but Tanner was nearly to the house.

"I apologize for my husband," Jules said when she rejoined Mac. "He has some issues from his childhood that he can't seem to deal with or get over."

Mac picked up the microphone to close the program, intending to forget what he'd heard. "We all have something," he told her before turning on the mic. "Don't worry about it."

But Jules wasn't the only one who'd noticed Tanner leaving. As friends and neighbors gathered around the boys, chatting and congratulating them on a job well done, Nikki walked up to join Mac, a slight frown on her face.

"Did Tanner leave?" she asked, searching the crowd.

Jules, standing nearby, joined them. "He had a call

he had to take." She glanced at Mac and shook her head when Nikki's attention was diverted. "He'll be back soon, I'm sure."

"You certainly surprised us, Nikki," Mac said, changing the subject. "Very impressive riding."

"The boys have been nagging me about what they refer to as my 'trick riding.' Maybe someday I'll show them the real stuff. But for now, they have something to work toward."

Before Mac could comment, Bridey walked up and announced there were refreshments. "Be sure to get a piece of the special cake for the boys," she told them.

Mac noticed that Nikki was surrounded by guests, praising her and the boys. It was her moment, hers and the boys, and he couldn't have been prouder of all of them.

"YOU'VE MET Kate and Trish, haven't you?" Jules asked, opening the door and stepping inside the white, two-story farm house.

Nikki followed her into the home of Kate McPherson, one of Jules's closest friends. "Yes, at the fall festival and today at the boys' riding exhibition."

Kate appeared in the entryway. "Wonderful! I'm so glad you decided to join us, Nikki." She looped her arm with Nikki's and led her away. "We try to do this once a month. It's our ladies' day in, our time to get away from the guys and the kids."

"Are your twins awake?"

"Tyler and Travis are at Trish's, with Krista. One of the high school girls is there with them," Kate explained.

"I still can't believe you both had your babies on the same day."

"It's Trish's fault," Kate said. "All the excitement of Krista's birth put me into labor."

"It was perfect timing for Paige," Jules chimed in.

"This is so beautiful," Nikki said as they stepped into a brightly lit room, filled with flowers and plants.

"Dusty added it onto the house last fall, while I was busy with wedding plans. He's become quite the do-it-yourselfer since retiring from bull riding." She picked up a remote control from one of the glass-topped tables and held it up. "I can even bring shades down at the touch of a button. They help keep the room cool in the heat of the day."

Nikki was in love with the room. "I'd spend every minute out here."

Jules laughed. "Oh, believe me, she does."

Kate nodded, laughing, too. "Every chance I get. But let's go sit on the deck. Trish is out there."

Nikki stepped through the glass French doors Kate opened for them and walked out into the September evening. Trish Rule, seated in a large, white wicker chair, waved to them. "Hi, Nikki! I'm glad you joined us today. We enjoyed the riding exhibition this afternoon. You've done wonders with those boys."

Nikki's heart filled with pride as her cheeks heated with a blush. "Thank you. They worked very hard, so it was easy for me. And thanks for including me tonight. I'm glad I came."

Jules and her friends had treated her as if they'd known her forever, the moment they met. That sort of thing seemed to come with the territory around Desperation. Since she'd arrived, everyone had been kind and welcoming. But she wasn't so sure that would be true if they knew who she was. Sally wasn't a favorite among the O'Briens, and more than likely the community felt the same way. She couldn't blame them, but her mother had changed, and she hoped would someday be forgiven.

"Paige said she'd be a little late," Jules said, settling onto a chair next to Trish, who turned to Nikki.

"Have you met Paige?"

Taking the seat across from her, Nikki shook her head. "No, I haven't."

Kate poured tea over ice in a glass and handed it to her. "Oh, you'll love her. She's Desperation's doctor."

"And our city attorney's sister," Trish said. "He's single, by the way," she added with a wicked grin.

"And good-looking," Kate chimed in.

"We'll introduce you to him as soon as we get a chance," Jules finished with a wink.

Nikki couldn't keep from laughing. "I see you're all in the matchmaking business."

"Kate and I inherited it," Trish told her. "It's in our genes."

Kate nodded. "Good old Aunt Aggie," she said with a chuckle. "One way or another, she was going to get me married off to Dusty or die trying, no matter how much I didn't agree with the idea." She spun around to face Trish. "Don't you dare tell her I used the word *old*."

They all burst out laughing. "I swear," Trish answered, making an *X* on her chest with her finger. "But it took both Aunt Aggie and Hettie to bring Morgan around."

"And you," Kate reminded her.

Trish leaned back in her chair and sighed. "Seems like a lifetime ago." She turned to Jules. "What about Beth? Is she going to make it tonight?"

Jules shook her head and settled on the chair next to Nikki. "She and Michael had things to do," she said, turning to Nikki. "While we're letting you in on how we nabbed our husbands—or they nabbed us—I should tell you that it was Beth who introduced me to Tanner."

"Beth Weston, the veterinarian?"

"One and the same. We became best friends when we were twelve. Then, too," she went on, smiling at Kate, "Dusty had a hand in it, although some would argue that he was pushing in the opposite direction."

"Apart?" Nikki asked, looking from one woman to the other.

Jules wrinkled her nose. "Not really. He just told me how it was with rodeo and let me take it from there. He was right. But to be honest, it was Shawn who stepped in and gave the last push that led us to take the big step."

A few moments of silence followed, and Nikki suspected that each of them was thinking about the not so distant past, wondering what might have happened if something—anything—had been different. She often wondered the same about her own life.

"I wanted to tell you, Nikki," Kate said, breaking the silence, "I enjoyed watching you ride today. It was fabulous!"

Nikki felt her face heat with embarrassment again, but managed a smile. "Thanks. Pole bending is similar to barrel racing, which I did when I was much younger."

Jules slowly turned to look at her. "You're a barrel racer?"

"Past tense," Nikki assured her.

Trish leaned forward. "Where did you get that great costume you wore? It was beautiful. The beads, the feathers... Gorgeous."

Nikki knew she was cornered. She couldn't tell them it had belonged to her mother. "My grandmother made it. If you really liked it, there's a Native American celebration scheduled for next weekend in Tahlequah." Feeling brave, she turned to Jules. "Maybe Tanner would like to see some Cherokee history."

Jules shook her head, and then let out a long sigh. "Tanner doesn't claim his Cherokee roots. He resents his Cherokee mother. She abandoned him, his younger brother and their father when Tanner was seven. He avoids anything connected to Cherokees or Native Americans."

Nikki's hopes evaporated. She'd suspected Tanner's life had been changed when their mother had left, but she hadn't expected he would feel the way he did.

"But he hired Nikki," Kate pointed out.

Nikki, feeling the sting of rejection her mother had warned her about, corrected her. "Jules hired me, not Tanner."

Once again they grew quiet, then Jules sighed. "I'm sorry, Nikki. It really isn't about you, just…"

Nikki understood completely. If she'd been in Tanner's shoes, she would probably feel the same. But she'd seen how Sally's choices had affected her life. She'd been young and hadn't realized that marriage wasn't a ticket to freedom and fun. Even as a small child, Nikki had seen the wanderlust in her mother's eyes when she talked about barrel racing. But Sally had left rodeo and become the kind of mother she knew she should have been from the beginning—sometimes to the extent of smothering. At least now Nikki knew why.

"Nikki?"

Looking up, she saw them all watching her. "I'm sorry. What were you saying?"

"We're going inside for some food," Kate said, standing.

Nikki nodded and followed them inside, but her thoughts were on Jules's revelation about Tanner. It made a difference. He might never accept her as his sister, considering how he felt about their mother. Rejection, she feared, was a sure thing, and it might be better if she gave more thought to telling him, at least for now.

Chapter Ten

"Come on. Get in."

Nikki stared at the classic red sports car and then at Mac. "Why?"

Mac had expected her to be surprised by the car, but he didn't think she'd be afraid of it. He also knew she'd insist on knowing how he could afford it on a wrangler's salary.

"I thought we'd take a ride," he answered.

She'd turned back to look at the car. "A ride to where?"

"Just a ride." He wasn't going to tell her where. She'd never get into the car if he did. Not that she seemed even tempted to. "It's a nice day," he said, keeping it simple. "Or haven't you noticed? And it'll do you good to get away from here for a while."

She took a step back, still gazing at the car, a frown on her pretty face. She turned to look at him, her eyes narrowed. "Whose car is this?"

"Mine." He always felt proud saying that and even more so at that moment.

"You stole it?"

His first reaction was to stare at her, but when he realized she was joking, he laughed. "Of course I didn't steal it. It's mine, so hop in and we'll take a spin."

"But where?"

His frustration climbed with each question she asked. "Does it matter where we're going?"

Her shoulders rose and sank in a slow shrug. "I guess not."

"Then get in," he said, opening the passenger door of the convertible for her.

"What about the boys?"

"Shawn's with them right now, throwing together a basketball game. And you know how Benito loves his basketball. We won't be gone all day."

After closing her door, he went around the front of the car, climbed in behind the wheel and started the engine. The sound of the motor calmed his exasperation. If nothing else, she'd enjoy a comfortable ride.

"Just out of curiosity," she began, "what kind of car is this?"

He smiled as he turned out of the drive and onto the county road, going slowly so the sand wouldn't damage his beauty. "It's a 1967 Austin-Healey 3000 Mk III BJ8."

"The name's bigger than the car."

He glanced at her, but she was looking straight ahead, her mouth still pulled down in a slight frown.

"You must be the richest wrangler I ever met," she said with a glance in his direction.

"I wasn't a wrangler when I bought it." He'd decided today wasn't going to be about him, so he changed the subject. "Better tie down your hair," he warned. "We're coming to the highway, and I'm not inclined to baby her today."

Once he was on blacktop, he pushed hard on the accelerator, pressing her back in her seat, her dark hair flying in the wind. "Don't you think you should slow down?" she asked.

"Believe it or not, we're under the speed limit."

All conversation stopped as he settled in his seat for the drive and noticed she did the same. The countryside around them was ablaze with the colors of autumn. The browns of tilled fields contrasted with the reds, oranges and yellows of the leaves still clinging to trees.

It wasn't long before they reached their destination. "Here we are," he announced, turning onto a long, rock-covered lane.

"Where's here?"

"Someplace I thought you might be interested in seeing." When she looked at him, he knew she hadn't seen the sign before they'd turned. "It's an EAP facility."

"Mac, I can't—"

"We're only visiting."

At the end of the quarter-mile lane he brought the car to a stop. As he got out, Nikki did the same, and they were greeted by a smiling, forty-something woman dressed in jeans, a denim shirt and boots.

"Mrs. Dayton?" he asked.

"Belle Dayton," she said, extending her hand, which he took. "You're just in time."

He introduced her to Nikki, and they followed the woman around a large barn to a corral where several teens were gathered in two groups. Two horses stood patiently nearby.

"Looks like a strategy session," Mac said.

"It is. They're working in teams," Mrs. Dayton explained.

"What's the objective?" Nikki asked.

Mrs. Dayton pointed to the corral. "Each team has

three minutes to get their horse to jump over the board that's across the two buckets."

"Seems simple enough," Mac said, glancing at Nikki.

A slow smile turned up the corners of her mouth. "Not at all simple." She turned to Mrs. Dayton. "Are there any rules?"

"Only a few. They can't touch the horse or bribe it in any way. They can't use anything outside the corral— no ropes, no halters. And once the one-minute strategy session is over, which I see it is, team members can't talk to one another."

"How long have they been at it?" Nikki asked, her attention on the activity in the corral.

"Both teams have had two tries. This will be their last."

Mac noticed that the members of one of the teams were smiling. When they broke up, one boy nodded to another, and the two of them moved in front of the horse. The rest joined in, and in a short time had moved the horse into a holding pen and closed it.

"They've got it," Mrs. Dayton said, excitement in her hushed voice.

The three of them watched as two of the boys picked up the board, while another picked up the buckets and placed them just outside the pen. The board was placed across them. Everyone in the group looked at each other, then one of the girls opened the pen. In unison, they began whistling. The horse, now attentive to what was going on, moved forward and jumped over the board.

Cheers went up from the winning group as the other team looked on, but frowns quickly turned to visible admiration, and the teens all shook hands. "We did it!" one of the boys called to Mrs. Dayton.

"I knew someone would," she said, flashing them all a victory sign with her fingers. She turned to Nikki. "Would you like to talk with the kids?"

Joy danced in Nikki's eyes as she nodded. "I'd love to."

Mac stayed at the fence, while Nikki followed Mrs. Dayton into the corral. Ten minutes later, as the group of teens started to leave, Nikki stood and talked with Mrs. Dayton privately. Mac wished he could hear the conversation. When he'd called to talk to Mrs. Dayton on Jules's recommendation, he'd asked if she would explain the EAP certification process to Nikki. She'd said she'd be more than happy to.

Mrs. Dayton and Nikki left the corral and joined Mac. When asked if they'd like something cold to drink, both Nikki and Mac accepted. Another half hour spent with Mrs. Dayton was filled with information. By the time they left, Mac felt certain Nikki was more than interested in learning more.

"So what did you think?" Mac asked as they drove home.

"It's fascinating," she answered. "I've always known how beneficial the interaction is between humans and animals, and what we saw today is proof of that."

She was in a good mood, giving him the perfect opportunity to plant the seeds. "Are you ready to start working on that certification?" She was quiet for too long, and he finally took his eyes off the road to look at her. "Nikki?"

She shook her head, refusing to look his way. "I can't," she said, her voice barely audible over the wind. "There are two strikes against me. The first is that I don't have the money needed for the seminars."

"That can be remedied. I'm sure Jules—"

"No."

"Okay," he said, refusing to argue with her. "What's the second reason?"

"I'd have to leave the Bent Tree." She turned to him, her smile sad and a bit wistful. "That's something I don't want to do."

"But…"

She shook her head again and turned to stare at the road ahead. "I appreciate the time and trouble you went to for the visit, but it isn't possible for me. And if you don't mind," she said, turning to look at him again, "I'd rather not talk about it."

All Mac could do was hope she would think it through a little more, but he didn't say anything. He wasn't going to argue. At the moment her mind—not to mention her heart—was made up.

THE MONTHLY SUNDAY BARBECUE for the boys was over, and after making sure all eight of them were in bed, Mac and Nikki headed back to the O'Briens' backyard.

"I hope Bridey has another dessert for us," Mac said, rubbing his palms together in anticipation.

"I can't decide which I like best," Nikki replied. "Bridey's Irish Jig or Kate's strawberry pie."

Mac peered at her in the evening light. "When did you have Kate's pie?"

"Last week after the boys' exhibition," she answered, rounding the corner of the house. "Kate McPherson invited me, and I went there with Jules."

"Yeah?"

She looked up at him and smiled. "Yeah."

"Lucky you."

"Good, you're back," Tanner said when they reached the patio. "Jules wants to discuss ways to raise money for the Bent Tree. She's checking on Wyoming, but will be right back. Have a seat."

Mac noticed that Nikki hesitated before settling on a chair across from Tanner. He was also aware that Tanner seemed to treat her a bit differently lately. And then he remembered what had happened during Nikki's riding exhibition and the little Jules had told him. He just couldn't believe Tanner would hold Nikki's heritage against her.

As if Tanner knew what Mac was thinking, he leaned forward in his chair. "I'm sorry I missed the end of your performance, Nikki. You're a fine rider."

"Thank you," she answered.

"Where did you learn pole bending?"

"A friend of my grandmother's taught me."

"Cherokee?"

Nikki nodded and answered, "Yes," but didn't elaborate.

"The Cherokee have a knack with horses," Tanner said, leaning back again. "At least, that's what I've been told."

"And he has a gold belt buckle to prove it," Jules said, joining them. "I'm glad you both could come back. The boys seemed a bit restless tonight."

"Nikki worked them hard this afternoon," Mac said, glancing at Nikki sitting beside him. "I think they were more tired than usual. It seems to bring out the devil in them."

"It definitely does with Wyoming," Jules replied.

But Mac was more interested in what her husband had mentioned. "Tanner said you're interested in raising money for the ranch. How can we help?"

"Cheryl Bickham mentioned that the state is seriously considering sending more boys. It's not official, but…"

"So where does the need for more money come in, specifically?"

"With more boys, we'll need more help," Jules answered. "I've interviewed several women I'd like to hire to help Nikki with the boys. I can only choose one, but that would free up both you and Nikki to concentrate more on the horses and the boys' riding. That would mean more horses, too, which don't come free." She glanced at her husband, but continued. "And an on-site counselor would be helpful. The boys are doing much better, now that Nikki is here. But it all means that the more boys we have, the more full-time help we'll need."

Mac gave the problem some thought. Having grown up in the marketing business, he knew that people tended to be generous, especially when it came to children. "Donations, if large enough, could help."

"But how do we get people to donate?" she asked. "There are good people in Desperation who would love to help, but the amount we need is far beyond their means."

"Advertising," he said. "Marketing." And then he saw the sly but hopeful look on her face. "You knew that, you deceptive woman. That's why you let me stay here and gave me a job."

"Heavens, no," Jules cried. "You know me better than that. I only thought of it the other day when I saw—" She jumped up from her chair. "There's something I want to show you. I'll be right back."

Mac looked at Tanner, who shrugged. "I don't know what it is. She didn't mention anything to me, but it has her excited."

Less than a minute later Jules returned with a newspaper in her hands. "I meant to show this to you, Tanner, but completely forgot." Instead of handing the paper to him, she gave it to Mac. "Take a look and tell me what you think."

He took it and leaned closer to the nearest light. There was an article written about the riding exhibition the boys had given. Lightly skimming the article, he noticed praise for the Bent Tree, its owners and Nikki. There was even a mention of him, although no name was given, but he didn't mind.

"What do you think?" she asked when he looked up from the paper.

"Was there a reporter here?" he asked.

"Apparently so. I have a hunch that may have been Hettie's doing. That's the Oklahoma City paper."

"This is the kind of thing that could become very advantageous for the ranch," he said, handing the paper back to her. "Build on it. If someone would be willing to form a foundation for donations and work to bring in people who could help, it might just get you the money you need."

"Really?"

"Yes." He glanced at Nikki, who sat silent beside him, taking it all in.

"I'll pay you well," Jules said, the sly look in her eyes returning.

Mac considered it. "I know you would, but…"

"Oh, Mac, please," she begged. "I know you're good at it. You know marketing from the bottom up."

"That's true," he answered, chuckling as he thought about the years he'd spent learning the business. "But if I do this, I'll need some help."

"Hettie," Jules answered quickly. "I'm sure she'd love

to be involved, and she has the contacts that could help." She took a deep breath. "And so do my parents."

"And mine," Mac added.

A smile brightened Jules's face. "Would you be willing to talk to Hettie about it, Mac?"

Surprised at how excited he felt at the prospect, he smiled. "I'll be happy to. Just tell me how to get in touch with her, and I'll do it first thing in the morning."

"I'll leave it in your hands, then."

They talked more about who else might be willing to get things rolling, and several names were brought up. But it wasn't long before they all decided to call it a night. Mac and Nikki thanked their employers for the evening. Hundreds of things ran through Mac's mind as they walked back to the main building, and adrenaline pumped through him. That's the way it always was when he faced a new opportunity. This felt right. His dad was one of the best in the marketing world, and Mac suddenly realized how lucky he'd been to be a part of it.

But he didn't want to go back to Boston—he wanted to stay here. He'd grown to love the ranch. And Nikki. He loved her patience, her kindness and her generosity. Trying not to had been a wasted effort—he knew that now. But there was one question in his mind. How did she feel about him?

Inside the building, he hesitated at his door when he noticed she hadn't gone to hers. His body hummed with having her near.

"Mac?"

Soft brown eyes gazed into his. He reached for her hand and gently pulled her closer. Hearing her soft sigh, he took her in his arms, tasting first one corner of her soft mouth, then the other. She melted into him, her arms slipping around his neck. He traced her lips with the tip of his tongue, and she opened them in response. He deepened the kiss, and his mind erupted in fireworks, while need burned through him. He held her even closer, molding her softness to his hard body.

It wasn't until Nikki slowly pulled away that he realized they were still standing in the hallway. "Good night, Mac," she whispered, stepping back and moving to her door.

He watched her slip inside her apartment. The question of how she felt about him had been answered.

NIKKI COVERED yet another yawn with her hand as Jules walked up to her in the barn. It was early evening, but she hadn't been able to sleep until the wee hours of the morning, excited that the Bent Tree would be growing.

"How did the trail ride go this morning with the boys?" Jules asked.

"Good," Nikki answered. "They really enjoyed the freedom to just ride. And they were starved when we got back, in spite of the big breakfast they'd had."

Laughing, Jules nodded. "That's boys. Always hungry. Jacob and Andrew seem to be adjusting well."

Nikki agreed. "Andrew is still a little shy with the others, but I suspect that won't last long. And although Jacob appears to be the serious type, he has a wicked sense of humor."

Jules nodded. "Never judge a book by its cover." She leaned back against the short wall of the stall Nikki was cleaning. "Do you realize it's been a month since you started working here?"

"A month?" To Nikki, it seemed like only a week or two, if that. But now that Jules had mentioned it, she realized much had happened in that month.

"As of this week, it's been a month," Jules said. "I meant to meet with you every week, but time flew by and there seemed to be no need to do it. I'm sure you know how pleased I am with your work."

"I couldn't ask for a better job," Nikki replied. "I love it here at the Bent Tree."

"Me, too," Jules said, laughing. But her laughter quieted as she studied Nikki. "Mac mentioned that he'd taken you to visit one of the EAP facilities."

"It was very interesting," Nikki admitted slowly.

"If Mac succeeds with the foundation to help with funding, I'd like to cover the cost to get you certified."

Nikki understood why Jules was willing to pay, but it didn't fix the other problem. "I'd have to leave the boys to do it, at least for a while," she explained. "And I just don't want to."

Pushing away from the wall, Jules straightened. "Mac told me about your concerns, and I understand how you feel about the boys. But you could help them and others even more if you'd attend the seminars. We can find some close by, so you wouldn't be gone for long periods."

Nodding, Nikki took a deep breath. "I'll certainly consider your offer."

"Good," Jules said. "And just so you know, I've hired a woman this morning. Her name is Linda Davidson— she was a teacher for many years before acquiring a nursing degree. She'll have a room in the main building, so we'll have someone here at all times who's licensed in health care. I'll introduce you when she arrives on Tuesday, and we'll do some brainstorming about sharing duties, as far as housemother is concerned. That should free up some of your time."

"I'll enjoy meeting her," Nikki replied, but she knew

she would miss any time she wouldn't be with the boys. Still, she'd have them for riding, so maybe it wasn't such a bad thing.

"I have phone calls to make," Jules told her, "so I'll see you in the morning, if I don't see you again later today."

"Thanks, Jules."

When Jules had gone, Nikki finished her work, made sure the boys were quietly occupied for the next hour and walked to the main building.

She was in the kitchen, reading a note from Bridey, when Mac walked in. "I decided it was time for a break," he said. "I see you did, too."

"Bridey left some chocolate cake," Nikki said, holding up the note.

"The Irish temptress," he said, reaching for the plastic cake holder on the cabinet. "Want to join me?"

She nodded and reached into the cabinet for two plates. "I think I will. I have an hour or so before I check on the boys again."

"If you'll cut us each a piece, I'll pour us some tea."

After settling on a nearby sofa in the commons, they were well into their cake when she spoke again. "You really had some great suggestions for Jules and Tanner last night."

He didn't look up from his plate. "I hope they help."

"Advertising and marketing are completely out of my realm. How do you know so much about them?"

He looked up at her, his eyebrows raised. "Digging for information?"

"Maybe."

Pushing his plate away, he leaned back. "Okay. I

guess it's time I revealed my deep dark secrets. Then you can share."

She nodded, but didn't say anything.

Mac continued. "A couple of months ago I received a letter from an attorney. It included a letter to me written by a man who claimed to be my biological father and who had recently died in prison."

Nikki leaned back and looked at him, unable to think of what she could say. "That must have been a shock."

He shrugged his shoulders and lifted his glass. "Apparently he liked to dabble in sharing stock information. That's major insider trading. Throw in some investment fraud and…" After taking a drink, he set the glass back on the small table. "I didn't know what to think. Nobody had ever told me the man who'd raised me had adopted me when he married my mother."

"So your mother is your biological mother."

"Yes. My biological father disappeared before she learned she was pregnant. After I was born, she married the man I'd always believed was my father, and he adopted me."

She was surprised. Adoption wasn't as shrouded in mystery and secrecy as it had been. Most children knew from an early age that they'd been adopted. "I'm sure they had a good reason."

Mac lifted his shoulders in a shrug. "I guess they believed they did. My dad is the owner of a major marketing firm in Boston. That's what Jules was talking about last night. I officially went into the business after college." He leaned back and rubbed his forehead with a fist. "I was angry when I learned they'd deceived me. I'm not who I thought I was."

Nikki could understand that he'd been upset. Anyone in that situation would feel the same. "But you're still the same person you were before you learned about the adoption."

He looked at her, shaking his head. "How can I be? The man I thought was my father isn't, and my parents kept that information from me."

"Parents are not always the people who gave life," she pointed out. But Mac didn't answer, and she decided it might not be the right time to talk about it. "So you left and came here?"

His mouth slanted in a wry smile. "Poor Jules. She was so surprised to see me at her door. To be honest, I probably didn't look all that great. She listened to my story, and then offered me the job. When I was a boy, I'd spent most of my summers at my godfather's ranch in Idaho. He taught me a lot about horses. But even before that, Megan was show jumping, and I did some riding, too."

"So that's why you know horses so well, but never struck me as a cowboy."

"Probably. I know I should forgive my parents for deceiving me all my life, but it isn't that easy."

Nikki picked up a small decorator pillow from the sofa and hugged it close. Her heart and mind warred. She'd done the unthinkable and fallen in love with Mac. How could she love someone, yet keep secrets from him? But how could she tell him? Deception was obviously something he didn't accept, and she'd been deceiving him *and* Tanner and Jules.

Standing, she tossed the pillow to the sofa. "I should be checking on the boys and reminding them it's bedtime."

Mac seemed deep in thought, but nodded. She wished she could do more for him. She didn't have to imagine how he felt, at least in one sense. She hadn't known her father, either—only that she had one she'd never met and, like Mac, would never know.

But she couldn't tell Mac that. Not yet. Not until she told Tanner. Sooner or later, he had to be told. But how would Mac feel when he learned she'd lied?

Chapter Eleven

"It's time," Mac said.

Nikki looked up from her breakfast plate. "Is he here?"

"He just arrived with the caseworker."

"Kirby?" she said, looking down the table at him. "It's time to leave." She stood and turned to Mac. Keeping her voice low, she asked, "Do you think it would be all right if I talk to him before he sees his father?"

Mac ducked his head before meeting her gaze. "I'm supposed to bring you both right away. They'll meet us at the house."

Nodding, Nikki saw the same apprehension in Mac's eyes that she was feeling. For Kirby's sake, she knew she had to at least appear positive, so she made sure she was smiling. "I'll meet you at the house in a few minutes, then," she told Mac.

She hurried to the main building and quickly let herself into her apartment. In her bedroom she pulled out a small tissue-paper-wrapped package, stuffed it into her pocket and then walked quickly to join the others at the O'Briens' home.

There was no need for anyone to tell her which person in the small group standing in the O'Brien living room was Kirby's father. The man was big. Tall and solid. His ebony skin matched eyes of the same color, and his smile appeared to be forced, especially when Nikki walked in and Jules hurried to introduce them.

"So this is who taught my boy to ride a horse," he said, taking the hand Nikki offered.

"He picked it up quickly." She added a smile that made her face hurt and pulled her hand away. His hand was the size of a side of beef, and she wondered just how much power it held.

Thankfully, Jules introduced her to the caseworker who would be supervising the visit. "Stephie Mullen," the young woman said.

"How long have you been with OKDHS?" Nikki asked.

"A month," Stephie answered. "It's been *so* rewarding."

She barely looked as if she was out of high school, but Nikki reminded herself not to judge. She, too, looked young for her age, and she hadn't been all that old when she'd first worked with Cherokee Nation Youth. But she'd worked in Intake, not as a caseworker.

"You'll excuse me, won't you? I have something for Kirby," Nikki said, and hurried to where Kirby stood with Mac and Shawn. When she looked at Mac, he immediately asked Shawn a question and led him a little away from Kirby.

Nikki knelt in front of the boy and reached into her pocket. "I have something for you," she said as she pulled out the small package.

He didn't smile, but he also didn't look as somber or stricken as he had in past days. "For me?"

She handed the gift to him. "It was my grandfather's," she explained while Kirby slowly opened it. "I never knew him. My grandmother gave it to me when I was about your age."

Kirby pulled off the last bit of tissue paper covering the silver-dollar-size polished piece of turquoise.

Seeing the spark of joy in his eyes when he looked up at her, she continued. "He meant to put it in a belt buckle, but he never did. When my grandmother gave it to me, she said it would bring me luck."

"Did it?"

"I'm here, aren't I?" she asked. He didn't speak, only nodded, and she wrapped her arms around him, pulling him close. "We'll be here for you tonight, Kirby," she whispered.

Leaning back, he looked at her, his dark eyes sparkling with happiness. "I know."

"We need to be getting home, boy," his father said, approaching them.

"Of course," she said, standing.

Kirby looked at her, and she gave him an encouraging smile. Hugging him again, she finally released him. "I'll walk out with you," she told them both, without looking at the man.

The caseworker stood at the door of her car and smiled at Kirby when the three of them reached the car. Nikki felt better for it. Jules, Shawn and Bridey joined them. Even Tanner, who carried little Wyoming, was there to send Kirby on his way.

"We'll see you tonight," Jules said as the Millers got into the car.

Apprehension mixed with sadness nearly brought tears to Nikki's eyes, but she managed to keep them at bay as the car drove away, Kirby sitting woodenly beside his father.

"I need to check on the other boys," she said, knowing

she had to get away before anyone noticed she was upset.

But as she stepped away, Jules pressed a hand to her arm. "Take the rest of the day off. I think we'll all join the boys for lunch, so don't you worry about it. I know what sleepless nights are like, and it looks like you could use some rest."

Nikki nodded and thanked her, but instead of going straight to her apartment, she checked on the boys first.

She discovered them playing basketball in the crisp fall weather, and watched them for several minutes. After making certain all was well, she went into the barn and went straight to work on the day's chores. She wanted to keep busy, not sleep, but it wasn't long before she found herself yawning. Putting the broom away, she walked to the main building.

Feeling lost in her small apartment, she picked up the letter her grandmother had sent and reread it. In it Ayita apologized in her spidery handwriting for telling Sally that Nikki was at the Rocking O.

Although her grandmother didn't go long into details, Nikki had discovered in the letter that Tanner's younger brother had visited her grandmother years ago. It had grieved Ayita not to tell her about the two boys, but Nikki understood, especially now that she knew the whole story.

Halfway through another reading that had her smiling again, there was a knock on her door. Placing the letter inside a book on the small table beside the sofa for safekeeping, she went to the door and opened it to find Mac on the other side.

"Are you okay?" he asked.

Just his asking made her eyes sting with tears, and she nodded. "Come on in."

"He'll be back tonight," he said, walking in to open his arms to her. "But if you want to cry, it's okay."

Without giving it a second thought, she stepped into his embrace and felt the warmth of his body next to hers. She sighed, then looked up at him. "I know you probably think I'm being silly and overprotective of him, but I'm too familiar with the system."

"How's that?" he asked, tracing his knuckles along her jaw.

Jolts of longing skipped through her, but she tried to ignore them. "When you need something done quickly, it moves with the speed of a turtle. But when you need things to go more slowly—" she took a deep breath "—it races with lightning speed."

He nodded when she looked up at him. "Most things do. Which is better?"

She knew he wasn't talking about the system, and she couldn't make up her mind. "I just need you. Here. Now."

She felt a chill when he released her, but he took her hand in his, and she led him to her bedroom. In the doorway of the tiny room he hesitated. "If this isn't the time—"

Smiling, she shook her head. "No way. But if you don't think—"

"Not on your life." He grasped the hem of her T-shirt and slowly pulled it over her head, then let her do the same for him.

She suddenly felt shy. It was the middle of the morning, and here they were, half-undressed. But she wasn't ready to stop, so she reached for the button on his jeans.

"Easy now," he said.

Neither of them heeded his warning, and they were soon in her bed, where he slowly explored her body, first with his hands, then with his mouth. He moved her beneath him, lifted her chin and gazed into her eyes. She didn't think she'd ever seen or felt anything so beautiful, and when his lips pressed hers, she gave herself up to his strength and comfort. Lifting her hips, she welcomed him.

MAC AWAKENED with Nikki snuggled next to him. He was tempted to stay and simply watch her sleep, but a glance at the clock on the bedside table told him he'd better get moving. It wouldn't be long before someone came looking for one of them, and the last thing he wanted was to be caught in a compromising position.

Quickly getting into his clothes, he moved silently, closing the bedroom door quietly behind him and stepping into the sitting room. But silence apparently wasn't the order of the day—he bumped the table by the sofa, and a book landed with a thud on the floor. Whispering a curse, he glanced at the bedroom door, praying the noise hadn't awakened her, before turning on the small table lamp so he could see what damage he'd done.

Papers that had apparently spilled from the book were scattered on the floor, and he bent to pick them up. He didn't mean to read them, but the faint handwriting caught his attention and the name "Sally" jumped out at him. Hadn't Tanner mentioned that name? He instantly remembered when.

Glancing again at the bedroom door, he read the letter addressed to Nikki more thoroughly. And wished he hadn't.

After putting the book back on the table with hands that shook, he placed the papers on top of it and squeezed his eyes shut. The urge to punch a wall hit him as the truth ripped through him. He'd trusted her. He'd fallen in love with her. Not only had his parents deceived him, but now Nikki had, too. She'd had every opportunity to tell him, but she hadn't. But it wasn't just about him. She'd lied to his friends. Her employer. Now it was about business. At any other time he wouldn't hesitate. He couldn't this time, either. Tanner and Jules needed to know and do whatever they felt was necessary.

The sun was low in the western sky before he finally went to the house. He was nearly there when he saw Bridey get out of a car and start up the walk. He heard her quiet laugh as the car drove away.

"Ah, there's that rascally Scotsman," she said, stopping to wait for him.

He didn't want to upset her, so he acted as if nothing was wrong, that nothing had happened to destroy the world he'd thought he was finally beginning to restore. "Did you enjoy your day?" he asked as they climbed the steps to the O'Briens' home together.

"It was charming," she answered, crossing the porch and opening the door. "Time with friends always is. Are you here to see Jules?"

He nodded. "And Tanner." *Especially Tanner.* "I have some information for them they asked me to check on." It wasn't completely the truth, but he didn't care.

Inside the house, Bridey cocked her head in the direction of the living room. "I don't hear anyone about. They're probably in Tanner's office. Jules goes in to interrupt his computer games nearly every evening."

Mac, filled with confusion and anger, couldn't comment as he followed her through the house.

At the office door Bridey knocked gently before opening it. "Mac is here to see you, Tanner," she announced.

"Thank you, Bridey," Mac said as he stepped into the room. When Bridey stepped back and closed the door, he took a deep breath, hoping it would calm him enough to say what needed to be said.

He could see Tanner behind his big desk, his booted feet propped on it, along with the computer screen at an angle on the corner. When Mac moved forward, Tanner dropped his feet.

Jules, sitting in one of the chairs across from Tanner's desk, looked up. "Is everything all right?" she asked.

Mac shook his head, then looked at Tanner. "I need to tell you something." He glanced at Jules. "Both of you."

"Sit down," Tanner said, nodding to the chair next to Jules.

Mac hesitated, then shook his head. "It's serious."

"I can see that. What is it?"

He walked closer to the desk and stopped. "Nikki has—" The words stuck in his throat, but he forced himself to continue. "She's…she's been deceiving us all."

Jules leaned forward, lines forming between her eyebrows. "Nikki?"

He turned to Tanner. "I don't know how to tell you this."

Tanner looked even more concerned than his wife. "Just say it, whatever it is."

Mac glanced at Jules. He didn't want to hurt either of them. Jules had been like a sister to him, and he knew that whatever hurt Tanner hurt her. She was…the best. And Tanner had become a close friend, giving him a job

at one of the worst times of his life and never questioning
him about it. He owed the man. And now he was going
to wound them both. It was the last thing he wanted to
do, but they needed to know.

Blocking all thoughts of the time he'd just spent with
Nikki, he did what needed to be done. "Apparently Nikki
is your sister."

Tanner stared at him across the desk. "No," he said.
"I don't have a sister. I have a brother." He closed his
eyes for a moment and lowered his head. "At least I hope
I still do."

"Your brother's name is Tucker."

"Yes."

"And your mother's name is Sally."

Tanner's eyes widened. But Mac wasn't finished.
"Sally is Nikki's mother. Brody O'Brien is her father."

Behind him, Jules gasped, but it was Tanner who
replied. "That's impossible."

"Why is it impossible?" Jules asked.

Tanner's jaw tightened. "Because it is. Sally left here
when I was seven, and I can assure you that she wasn't
pregnant."

"Can you?"

"Of course I can!"

"Maybe you should calm down," Jules suggested
quietly.

"I don't have a sister!" Tanner said, his voice echoing
in the room.

"I found a letter from her grandmother—your grand-
mother—apologizing for telling Sally where Nikki was,"
Mac explained. "It went on about Nikki's two brothers,
Tanner and Tucker."

"Impossible," Tanner stated.

"Tanner," Jules said, her voice quiet but firm, "listen

to him. You can't keep denying the past for the rest of your life. Unless you're reminded, you act as if Sally never existed. And then when you are reminded, it's as if she couldn't possibly have had a life after leaving here." She looked at Mac. "Where did you find the letter?"

Mac wasn't about to tell them why he'd been in Nikki's room. Knowing he'd been a fool didn't mean they needed to know just how big a fool. "I knew she was feeling down about Kirby leaving, so I went to check to see if she was all right. Her door was unlocked, and I found her sleeping. I also found the letter, completely by accident, as I was leaving. When I read what was in it—"

Jules jumped to her feet. "You read a personal letter?"

"I didn't mean to," he said in his defense, even though he knew it was wrong. "I'd knocked it on the floor, and when I picked it up to put it back on the table, some of the words just…jumped out at me." At least that much was true.

Tanner nailed him with his gaze. "Why is she here? Did you get a hint as to the reason?"

Mac shook his head. "There was nothing in the letter that alluded to a reason. Maybe she wanted money. It wouldn't be the first time something like that has happened."

Tanner turned to Jules. "You should have checked her out."

With her head held high, Jules took her seat. "I did. Was I supposed to get her pedigree? Find out who her family is, her parents' names? All applicants are thoroughly screened, as they are for any business. Do *not* lay this at my door."

Running his hand through his hair, Tanner sighed. "I'm sorry. You aren't to blame. I know you do a thorough job."

"And I'm sorry, too," Mac said. "The last thing I wanted to do is hurt either of you, but not knowing why she's here, I didn't want you to be blindsided when you discovered who she is. It would have happened, sooner or later, whatever her plans."

"We'll have to let her go," Tanner announced.

"We need to talk to her first," Jules countered, a stubborn tilt to her chin.

"Maybe you should go get her and bring her here."

Jules shook her head. "I— No. She'll know something's wrong as soon as she sees me, and I'm not going to be the one to condemn her, as you are."

"Jules—"

"I have her cell-phone number. I can call her and ask her to come to the house."

Tanner nodded. "If that's how you want to do it."

"I'll tell her," Mac said.

Tanner and Jules turned to look at him. "That isn't necessary," Jules assured him.

"It is," he answered. Jules didn't look convinced. "I won't say anything, only tell her she's wanted here."

Jules looked to Tanner, who shrugged. "All right," she said with a sigh. "If that's what you both think is best. But please treat her kindly. We don't know the whole story."

IT WAS GROWING DARK when Nikki opened her eyes and discovered that Mac had gone. Stretching, she smiled. It was wrong to do what they'd done, especially here in her room, but she didn't regret it. And no matter what happened next, she never would.

Finally rested, she climbed out of bed, a stab of guilt for sleeping so long hitting her. She slipped into her clothes, but feeling a chill in the air, she exchanged her T-shirt for a short, wooly sweater. Still smiling, she ran a brush through her long hair, then went into the sitting room, wondering if she should find something to eat.

But she wasn't hungry. Not for food, anyway. Instead, she grabbed the throw on the back of the sofa and snuggled under it. She reached for her grandmother's letter, but noticed it was no longer in the book where she'd put it. Before she could wonder why, there was a knock on her door.

She smiled when she saw Mac standing in the hallway. "Back so soon?" she asked, teasing, and opened the door wide.

"Tanner and Jules would like to see you."

His voice was hard, but held no emotion. Tilting her head to the side, she looked at him. "Is something wrong?"

Instead of answering her question, he said, "They're in Tanner's office."

"All right." She didn't know what this was about, but there was definitely something wrong with Mac. Her heart leaped to her throat, and her hand flew to her mouth. *Or Kirby.* "Is Kirby—"

"As soon as possible."

"But…"

His blue eyes hardened. "Kirby's fine."

Nodding, she glanced around the room, taking it all in, as if it would give her an answer. Something was wrong—terribly wrong—and it seemed Mac wasn't willing to tell her.

Stepping out into the hallway, she closed the door behind her, ready to ask why Tanner needed to see her. But Mac was acting so strangely and was already half-way down the hall.

Once outside, she had to run to try to keep up with him, and by the time she did, they were in the house at the door to Tanner's office.

"Are you coming in, too?" she asked, a little out of breath.

Instead of answering, he tapped lightly on the door. From inside, she heard Jules's voice telling them to come in.

Nikki's gaze went immediately to Tanner, who sat behind a large wooden desk, his hands clasped on top of it. When the door clicked behind her, she turned, expecting to see Mac, but he wasn't there. She caught sight of Jules, sitting in a high-backed wing chair, across from Tanner's desk.

Clearing her throat, she tried to smile. "You wanted to see me?"

"Please sit down, Nikki," Jules said.

Nikki walked to the chair next to her, but didn't sit. Something wasn't right. "N-no, I'll stand, if you don't mind."

"Why are you at the Rocking O, Nikki?" Tanner asked, a harsh quality in his voice she'd never heard.

"I'm here because—" A vision of Ayita's letter, on top of the book by her sofa, flashed through her mind. She hadn't left it there, she was sure. She'd put it in the book when Mac had come to the door, and he'd gone while— "Oh, my," she whispered, and sank into the chair behind her.

She turned to look at Jules, who, for the first time Nikki could remember, looked confused and distraught. "Would you mind answering the question?" Jules asked, glancing at Tanner.

Nikki nodded slowly. Her life at the Bent Tree was over, of that she was certain. She'd come under false pretenses, but not to hurt anyone. She'd wanted only to meet her brother.

Lifting her head high, as her grandmother would expect her to do when admitting a wrong, she answered. "I came here for two reasons. The first was to help children." She glanced at Jules, who gave her a small but sad smile. "The second reason," she said, turning to Tanner, "was to get to know you."

"What else?" he answered, his frown formidable.

"Nothing more than that."

"I don't believe you."

His words were like a slap in the face. She'd always been honest, and in time she had hoped to tell him who she was. "I'd like to explain," she said.

Before Tanner could answer, Jules did. "I'd like to hear it."

Nikki searched for the right words to tell her story, even knowing it wouldn't help. "As you both know, I'm half Cherokee." She saw a slight flicker cross Tanner's face, but ignored it and continued. "I spent my early childhood with my Cherokee mother. I didn't know who my father was until I was thirteen."

"And now you're claiming—"

"Hush, Tanner," Jules told him. "Let her finish."

Nikki didn't look at him. He'd already guessed what she was going to say. Mac had obviously told them both. Knowing that broke her heart. But there wasn't time to examine it. Jules and Tanner needed to hear it from her, not as an accusation.

"My parents were married, but..." She took a deep breath and forced herself to stand. "My mother wasn't bad. She was young, headstrong and self-centered, and she's lived with the guilt of what she did."

She glanced at Tanner. His eyes were narrowed and he was frowning, but it was his hands gripping the chair that drew her attention.

She couldn't stop now. She had to finish and tell him. Wrapping her mind around the happy ending she'd imagined, she took a deep, shaking breath. "I hope you can forgive her someday. And forgive me, too."

"No."

"Sally Rains is my mother, Tanner. Brody O'Brien is my—"

"That's not possible."

"Listen to her, Tanner," Jules said.

"I don't need to," he answered, standing. "This is a crazy story, something she made up. I don't have a—"

"A sister," Jules finished for him. "And maybe you don't or maybe you just never knew. If you'd just listen."

Standing in front of Tanner, Nikki had never felt so alone or so lost. Even Jules had accusation in her eyes, although she was kind enough not to voice it.

"I'm sorry you don't believe me," Nikki said, "or think that I'm here for anything other than what I've told you. I know how hard it must have been for you when Sally left. It was shameful, and I can understand how you felt and still feel. But she changed. When she left here, she didn't know she was pregnant with me. She tried..."

Tears threatened in the silence of the room, but she

forced herself to be strong. "She called here when I was two. She asked to see you and Tucker, but a woman answered and refused to tell her anything. She told my mother never to contact or try to see you." Closing her eyes, she prayed for strength. "She never did again."

When she opened her eyes, Tanner started to speak, but Nikki wasn't finished. "I was wrong to deceive you, to not tell you. My mother warned me that we weren't wanted here. I thought—" She shook her head. "I knew there was a chance you would turn me away, but I thought maybe if you had the chance to get to know me first…"

Jules stood and glanced at Tanner. "Let's save this for tomorrow. Tanner is—"

"I'd like you to leave, Nikki," Tanner said as if he hadn't heard his wife. "Jules can send you whatever pay she owes you, but—"

Jules took a step forward. "You can't do that," she told him. "I hired her."

Nikki had had enough punishment for one night. She would never quit blaming herself, her pride, her desire to know her family. She'd known the second she realized why she'd been called to Tanner's office that she wouldn't be wanted.

Without another word she walked to the door and slipped out of the room. She'd taken only a few steps when she realized the enormity of the situation. She'd never see Kirby again. She'd never be able to protect him, to give him a hug.

Through the tears in her eyes she saw Mac standing in the hallway. His face was like a mask, revealing nothing. Squaring her shoulders, she kept walking. He would never know that he had destroyed her. But in a dark, secret part of her heart, she knew she had been the destroyer by not being honest.

When she reached him, she stopped, praying she wouldn't cry in front of him. "Tell Kirby…" She took a deep breath. "Tell him he'll be okay. Look after him, Mac. He trusts you."

Chapter Twelve

Mac stared after Nikki as she left the house. A part of him wanted to go to her and ask for forgiveness, but he couldn't. She'd fooled them all, deceived them, just as his parents had deceived him.

Pushing away from the wall, he turned for the office. It was obvious that Nikki was leaving. His mind raced back to the night he'd helped her unload her belongings from her car, but he forced it from his mind. Now was not the time to think about it. There would probably never be a time when he wanted to revisit the past few weeks.

"Back again, are you?"

The soft Irish lilt told him Bridey was behind him, and he turned to see her coming from the kitchen, carrying two coffee cups. "More like still here," he answered, stopping to wait for her.

"I'll have to get another cup for you, but—"

"There's no need for that. I can get my own if I need it."

She smiled. "I've heard the Scots can be quite pleasant and helpful at times."

Mac shook his head and chuckled, putting aside the reason he was there. "I hate to put a halt to the fun,

Bridey, but I'm not the Scotsman you think I am. I'm only Scottish by name, not by birth."

One thin eyebrow lifted. "So you say? Well, there's no matter. We can still be friends."

They walked to the office together, Bridey talking about how she'd always known, while Mac heard only a part of what she said. When they reached the door, Mac tapped on it for her, and then opened it to let her pass in front of him.

At first glance, he noticed that Jules was standing by the window, looking out, while Tanner was still at his desk. Neither was speaking. "Are we intruding?" he asked.

"Not at all," Jules said, turning to glance at her husband. "Come in, both of you, and sit down."

He looked at Bridey, not knowing if he should speak about what had gone on before, before asking, "You fired her?"

"Of course," Tanner answered.

Jules ignored her husband. "Because Tanner can't let go of a lifelong grudge."

"She abandoned us, Jules!" Tanner said, his face drawn with emotional pain. He stood and walked toward his wife. "How do you think I should feel?"

"And Nikki had what to do with that?" Jules asked.

"She never tried to see us, never called again to see if we were all right. I was seven years old!"

His words hung in the air until a voice not yet heard from spoke. "It's my fault."

They all turned to look at Bridey, who sat on one of the chairs, a tear sliding down her usually rosy cheek. "What?" Tanner asked.

"Sally called once," she said, wiping the tear away. "It was a year or two after she'd left, maybe a little longer.

She wanted to come see you boys. I thought she wanted to come back." She shook her head. "I didn't give her the chance to say so. I told her you and Tucker were fine, and you didn't need her. I insisted she never call again and that she never try to contact either of you or try to see you. I said I would call the sheriff and have her taken away if she did."

Tanner ran a hand over his face. "You never said anything."

Bridey looked from Jules to Mac to Tanner. "Pride can make a person do and say things they shouldn't. I was angry with her, and maybe a little jealous. I didn't want to share you boys with anyone. Not even your mother."

Jules moved to kneel beside Bridey's chair. "She didn't say anything about a daughter?"

Sniffing back tears, Bridey shook her head. "I never gave her a chance."

Nodding, Jules held her hand. "It's all right, Bridey. I understand why you did it. You thought you were protecting the boys."

"But it was wrong," Bridey answered. Her eyes shimmered with more tears. "How can I ever make it up to you, Tanner?"

He moved to where she sat with Jules and leaned down, close to her. "There's no need to do that. You did it out of love." Reaching into his pocket, he pulled out a handkerchief and handed it to her.

She gave him a watery smile and took it, dabbing at her eyes.

Stunned, Mac didn't know what to think. "I guess I don't know what's going on," he admitted. "And maybe it's none of my business…"

"Tanner?" Jules asked, looking at her husband.

Tanner nodded. "He deserves to know." Turning to Mac, he sighed. "I don't know where to begin, but I may have done Nikki a disservice."

Mac didn't believe anyone had done anything wrong except Nikki, but he was willing to listen. "So what's the story?"

Tanner settled on his desk. "It's a long one, but if you're willing to hear it…"

Mac nodded. Maybe it would clear up a few questions he had.

"My dad, Bridey's twin brother, was a bull rider. He fell in love with a young Cherokee girl and wanted to marry her, but her parents felt she was too young, so they told him they would give their blessing when she turned eighteen. They may have hoped the attraction would wear off. I don't know. But as soon as she was eighteen, Brody and Sally married."

"Too many people marry too young," Mac said.

Tanner glanced at his wife. "Brody bought the land that's now the Rocking O, built this house, although a bit smaller, and moved his new wife here. Within a year, she had me. But she was a barrel racer and all she wanted was to rodeo. When I was two, she disappeared, but Brody quickly found her on the rodeo circuit and brought her home. Her parents weren't happy, from what I've been told, but they'd warned him that she was young when he'd married her. A year later my brother, Tucker, was born. Sally stayed for a few years, and then left again. I was seven by then, and Tucker was four. I've never seen her since then."

"Wow," Mac said. "A mother who left her children. That had to be hard for you to deal with." At least he hadn't been abandoned. In fact, quite the opposite.

"Bridey came to live with us, and my dad left to ride

the rodeo circuit, thinking that's where Sally had gone. But he died when a bull's hoof connected with his head. I was fourteen by then, and tried to help Bridey raise Tucker." Tanner shook his head. "That was probably the worst thing I ever did."

"Jules told me your brother left when he was... fifteen?"

Tanner nodded, but said nothing else.

"So Nikki *is* your sister?"

"It certainly seems that way."

Jules quickly gave her opinion. "There's no doubt in my mind that she is."

Out of the corner of his eye Mac saw Bridey get to her feet.

"I can give you proof," she said, "if you'll wait a minute or two."

Mac was stunned and noticed Jules and Tanner were, too, as Bridey hurried out the door. Tanner paced the length of the room, while Jules simply watched him, a curious expression on her face.

"You know," she said, looking first at Tanner, then at Mac, "the two of you are quite the pair."

"What do you mean?" Tanner asked.

"You, Mac," she said, pointing a finger at him, "have it in your head that Nikki was after something. Do you really think she wanted money?"

Mac stared at her. "I don't know. All I know is that she wasn't honest, and that always leads to other things."

She stared back. "Always?" But before he could answer, she turned to Tanner. "And you." She shook her head. "You seem to believe she made up the story about being your sister. Did either of you think that you both might be wrong?"

They were saved from answering when Bridey

returned with a photo frame in her hand. "'Tis my mother," she announced, handing the frame to Tanner. "Your grandmother."

Tanner looked at the picture, his eyes widening. "Those eyes… And that *mouth*." He looked at Jules. "All right, you win. She wasn't lying about being my sister. But that doesn't excuse the fact that she wasn't honest about it."

"And I don't blame her for that," Jules answered, and returned to her chair.

Mac turned to Bridey. "You knew it the minute you saw her."

"I suspected," Bridey admitted. "At first. But it wasn't long before I was certain."

"Why didn't you say something?" Tanner asked.

Bridey's smile was sad. "Because for once, I wasn't going to step in where I shouldn't."

No one spoke for a moment, and then Mac broke the silence. "It's her deception that bothers me," he admitted. "I don't know if I can forget about that."

Jules looked at him, her smile filled with regret. "She had good reason," she said, glancing at her husband. "I hope that in time—"

She was interrupted by the telephone ringing. "It could be Nikki, although I doubt it," she said.

Nodding, Tanner grabbed the phone, but Mac could tell by the way he answered that the call wasn't from Nikki. Tanner handed the phone to Jules.

"This is Jules O'Brien," she said, then fell quiet. "Oh, dear. Yes, I understand. We'll be there as quickly as possible. And thank you."

"Who was it?" Tanner asked.

Mac felt a ton of weight hit him. "Is it Kirby?"

Jules nodded. "He's been taken to the hospital. They'd like for us to come."

"Where's his father?" Mac asked.

Jules didn't look at him. "They… They didn't say, exactly."

Tanner looked at his watch. "You're going to Oklahoma City?"

Jules nodded.

"It's late, so the traffic won't be bad. We should make good time."

"I'm going, too," Mac announced. Nikki had asked him to look after the boy, and even though he was still reeling from her deception, he wouldn't let Kirby down. "I'll drive."

"All right," Tanner said, and turned to Bridey. "Can you stay here with the boys?"

"Linda Davidson will be here in the morning," Jules reminded them. "If we're not back, I'm sure she can help. You can explain what's happened."

Bridey nodded. "I'm happy to watch the boys. It's what I do best."

While Jules explained what might need to be done during their absence, Tanner grabbed his keys and tossed them to Mac. "You get the truck," he told him. "I'm going to call Morgan and see if he can give us some assistance. Meet me out front."

"He's in here," the nurse said, leading them to one of the examining rooms.

"Thank you," Jules said.

Behind her, Mac's body still hummed from the adrenaline of the drive. It hadn't taken them as much time as he'd thought it would, but then he'd broken most of the speed limits. He hadn't been stopped, though. Morgan had led the way, lights flashing.

"Kirby, are you okay?" he heard Jules ask as Mac stepped into the room.

Kirby, looking even smaller than usual, sat on the padded examining table, his left arm in a sling. "I have a broken arm," he announced with a small smile. But the smile widened when he met Mac's gaze. "Hi, Mac."

"How're you doing?" Mac asked, stepping closer.

"Okay. Where's Nikki?"

Mac looked at Jules, who said nothing, but the look on her face said it was his fault, and he'd have to live with the consequences. "She—she couldn't come with us."

"Is she sick?" Kirby asked.

It was more than he'd heard from Kirby since he'd started work at the ranch. Unfortunately it wasn't the best time to be asking questions. The only answers Mac had would just upset the small boy.

The door opened and a man Mac suspected was the doctor stepped in. "Mrs. O'Brien, can I speak with you?"

Jules nodded, but turned to Kirby. "You stay here and talk to Mac. I'll be back in a few minutes."

When she was gone, Mac moved closer to Kirby. "Does it hurt?"

Kirby shrugged. "It did, but they gave me some medicine and said I'd feel better."

"How did you break it?"

Kirby didn't answer immediately, and didn't look Mac in the eye when he finally did. "I fell."

Mac didn't believe him. It was the same answer he'd given when Nikki had asked about the scar on his cheek. "Just fell out of bed?"

Nodding, Kirby peeked up at him, and the nod changed to a shake of his head. "I was…jumping on the bed and fell off. I guess I fell on something."

Same story. But this time he'd added the bed jumping. Mac still didn't believe it.

"Mac?"

He turned around to see Jules in the doorway.

"Can you come out here for a second?"

Tanner appeared behind her. "I'll sit with Kirby," he said.

Mac nodded, then turned to pat Kirby's leg. "Stay right where you are, big guy. I won't be long. I promise."

"Over here," Jules called to him when he stepped into the hallway.

"I'm Dr. Stewart," the man with her said. "Mrs. O'Brien wanted you to see the X-rays of Kirby's arm."

Mac followed them down the hall to an X-ray panel. He wasn't sure how much he could tell from a picture of some bones, but he wasn't going to argue.

The doctor flipped a switch, and a soft, fluorescent light came on. Mac looked at the X-rays clipped to the front of the light box.

"See that?" the doctor said, pointing to a place in what looked like the middle of an upper arm.

"It isn't straight," Mac said, puzzled by the look of the bone.

"It's called a spiral fracture," Dr. Stewart explained. "We see them too often, especially with smaller children. Did Kirby mention how his arm was broken?"

Mac shrugged. "He said he was jumping on the bed and fell, but I don't believe that."

"Good. I'm glad you're questioning it." He looked at Jules, then turned back to Mac. "This kind of fracture is usually a good sign that there's been abuse."

Mac suddenly felt sick to his stomach. Both he and Nikki had suspected there'd been things that had happened to Kirby that he wasn't willing to talk about. This was the proof.

"I'll show you how the fracture occurs." The doctor took Mac's upper arm and wrapped his fingers around as much as possible. "Obviously I can't show you exactly," he said with a grim smile. "You're much bigger than a child. But a spiral fracture is caused when the arm is twisted...like this."

He attempted to do the same to Mac's arm to show how it was done, and Mac winced. "I see," he said rubbing where the doctor had twisted his arm. He turned to Jules. "Somebody is looking into this, aren't they?"

"His father has been picked up and is claiming he didn't do it."

"What about the caseworker? Where the hell was she?" Mac demanded furiously.

Sighing, Jules led him away from the X-ray. "She told the dispatcher that she'd stepped out to use her cell phone. There wasn't reception in the apartment building."

Mac gritted his teeth. This was unbelievable. "Who was she talking to on her phone? Her boyfriend?"

Jules shook her head. "She has a baby at home, and she was trying to reach the babysitter to make sure everything was okay."

Mac felt like a heel. "Oh. So where is she now?"

"She rode here in the ambulance with Kirby. She was so upset about what happened that as soon as she gave her statement to the police, she was given a sedative. She's in a room here, overnight."

Nodding, Mac glanced at the door of the room where Kirby waited. If Nikki had been here, she'd— But she wasn't, and that was his fault. "So what are we going to do?"

"I'm going to be making some phone calls. I want assurances that Kirby will be going home with us."

"He won't be going back to his father?"

"It's highly unlikely," she answered. "And maybe you can help. If you can get Kirby to tell you the truth about how his arm was broken—and like you, I believe it was his father who did it, just the way the doctor showed you—then he'll never be allowed to see Kirby again."

Mac thought long and hard about how he might be able to get Kirby to tell him. He wasn't nearly as good at these things as Nikki was, but he was more than willing to give it a try, especially if it meant Kirby would be taken from the brute who'd hurt him.

"All right," he told her. "I'll do what I can."

"And I'll do what I can on the legal end of it."

When he stepped into the examining room, Mac found Tanner telling Kirby about how he'd won his gold belt buckle at National Finals Rodeo a few years before. Kirby was enthralled, but when he looked up at Mac, he beamed.

"Did you talk to Nikki?" he asked as Tanner left the room.

The weight in the pit of Mac's stomach only got heavier. "Not yet, champ." He still wasn't ready to forgive Nikki and wasn't sure he ever would, but he wished she was the one handling this, not him.

Kirby's smile had dimmed. "Can we go home now?"

Mac walked to where the boy sat and put his arm around him. "Not quite yet. We're waiting to find out what we have to do next."

And Mac didn't have a clue how to get him to tell

the truth about how his arm had been broken. And then he remembered that he'd built a little trust with Kirby over Nikki's missing ring. He could do this if he tried. He'd find out what happened, and Kirby would be able to go home with him. He just didn't want to think about what Kirby would do when he discovered Nikki wasn't there.

Grabbing a chair, he turned it around and placed it in front of Kirby, then straddled it so he could look up at the boy, not tower over him. "Kirby," he said. "I need you to do something for me."

"What?"

"I need you to be honest with me." Instead of answering, Kirby blinked. Mac tried to think of how Nikki would handle it. "You trust me, don't you, Kirby?" he asked.

Kirby nodded. "I trust you and Nikki and Jules and Tanner and Shawn and Shamar and Leon and—"

"Good, good," Mac said before Kirby could list the rest of the boys. "And you know that we all care about you very much. We love you."

"Even Shamar and Leon and—"

"Even them. Not that they'll tell you in so many words, but remember how Shamar helped you with your saddle?"

Kirby nodded. "I didn't even have to ask him—he just did it."

"Right." Mac tried to choose his words carefully. "And now you can help us. Will you do that?"

"I guess."

Mac hoped it would be more than a halfhearted attempt by Kirby. They needed to know the truth. "I want you to be honest with me, okay?" Kirby nodded, but it definitely wasn't with vigor. "When you told the hospital people that you hurt your arm when you fell off the bed, was that the truth?"

Kirby lowered his head and said nothing for several seconds.

"We need to know if something else happened," Mac told him. "Do you understand?"

Nodding, Kirby lifted his head. His dark eyes were filled with fear and sadness, but he nodded. "It was him."

"Him?" Mac didn't want to put words in the boy's mouth. Kirby needed to say it.

"My dad."

Relief washed through Mac, but it wasn't over. "How did he do it, Kirby?"

"He— He was mad 'cause I said I was hungry."

Mac cringed, but said nothing. Hadn't Nikki already gone over this? Was there never food available for him in his own home?

"He always gets mad when I say that," Kirby continued, "and he grabbed my arm and jerked me up in the air. It hurt. Bad. I guess that's when my arm broke."

Mac couldn't speak, but he knew he had to assure Kirby that telling him was the right thing to do. "I'm sorry that happened, buddy," he said, reaching up to cup his face in his hand. But Kirby jerked away, as if Mac was going to hit him. "Whoa! It's okay, Kirby. I'll never hit you."

"I didn't mean to—"

"I know," Mac answered. "But I need to ask you two more questions, okay?" When Kirby nodded, Mac went on. "Can you tell the people who need to know so they can help you? Can you tell them what really happened, how you broke your arm?"

The boy seemed to consider it. "As long as he won't hurt me for telling."

"He won't hurt you again, Kirby, I promise." Not when Kirby was willing to tell the people who could help. But he still wasn't finished. "That scar on your face. Did your dad do that, too?"

Without hesitation, Kirby nodded.

"Why didn't you tell Nikki and me that when she asked?"

Kirby shrugged. "Because I didn't know how, and he said if I told anybody, he'd hurt me again."

That was all Mac needed to hear. He stood. "I need to let Jules know what you've told me. Is that okay?"

Nodding, Kirby still looked a little wary. "Can we go home now?"

"Let me check with Jules and the doctor. Will you be okay in here by yourself?"

"As long as you come back soon."

Mac smiled, but his heart ached for the boy. "I will."

He stepped out of the room and searched for Jules. Finding her as she was finishing a call, he approached her. "Kirby is ready to tell what happened. And he wants to know when he can go home with us."

Jules still maintained the cool assuredness of an attorney. "He can come with us. It's temporary, but I'm working on that. The doctor said the swelling in Kirby's arm needs to go down before they cast it. Thank goodness he doesn't think it needs surgery! He said we could take Kirby home if we're very careful. They'll put on a half-cast splint and wrap it. He won't need to come back here to the hospital. In a couple of days Paige can put a real cast on the arm."

"That's good," Mac said. "I need to let him know."

Back in the room, he gave Kirby the good news. Although the boy seemed to be happy, his smile wasn't as bright as Mac thought it might be.

"What is it, Kirby?" he asked, pulling him close, but being careful of the arm.

One fat tear rolled over the scar on Kirby's cheek. "I want Nikki."

Mac thought his heart was breaking. "I know you do."

Kirby looked up at him. "If my dad isn't going to be my dad anymore, can you and Nikki be my mom and dad?"

Mac didn't have an answer. So much had happened in the past twenty-four hours, he didn't know how he felt anymore. And he didn't know when he would. For now he was numb.

Chapter Thirteen

"Where are you going, Nioka?"

Nikki let go of the door and turned to look at her grandmother. "To the school to talk to Charlie Bright-water. I'm hoping he'll give me back my old job."

Ayita Rains nodded. "But why there? Why not with Youth Services? You enjoyed helping the children there."

Nikki had considered it over the past week since she'd left the ranch. She missed the boys. She missed every-one. But it was time to put it all behind her. Working at Youth Services would only be a reminder of the boys. "Because I'd rather return to Sequoyah Schools."

Her grandmother sighed. "Come. Sit by me."

After having avoided anything more than a quick chat with her grandmother since arriving, Nikki knew there were questions to be answered. She'd told her grand-mother very little, thinking it would be better. "Can we do this later?" she asked. "I don't want to be late."

"Charlie will wait. He's younger than I am."

Nikki couldn't stop her smile. While it was true her grandmother was nearing ninety, she was still as sharp as she'd been when Nikki was a child. That might not be such a good thing, Nikki thought as she moved to sit on the floor near her grandmother's chair, the spot she'd always taken when she was a young girl.

Ayita smoothed Nikki's hair with a gentle hand. "You haven't told me why you returned. Now would be a good time, I think."

Shrugging, Nikki took a deep breath. "It didn't work. I never should have gone there."

"Then you never would have met your brother."

"But it was just like Mom told me." She looked up to see her grandmother watching her closely, her eyes bright and knowing, and she had to look away, aware that tears would come when she spoke about what had happened. "They don't want me there. I deceived them. I should have told them from the beginning who I was."

"You would have been given the job if you'd done that?"

Nikki shook her head. "No."

"And you loved the job. You loved the boys you looked after."

Her throat thick with emotion, Nikki could only nod.

"People's hearts can change."

Not this time. "It doesn't matter," Nikki said, hoping saying it would make it true. She tipped her head up to look at her grandmother. "I don't want to be far from you."

"And my wish is for you to be happy."

"I will be, I promise." Nikki started to stand, but her grandmother's hand on her shoulder stilled her.

"Tell me what he's like."

"He looks like I expected," Nikki answered. "Tall, dark and handsome. And oddly, he has blue eyes. I guess the O'Brien recessive gene came through."

"One blue, two brown," her grandmother replied.

Nikki looked up at her. "How do you know?"

"I saw the boys when they were small. I remember Tucker's eyes. Tanner's, too. But I want to know what Tanner is like, not how he looks."

"He's very kind. The boys' ranch belongs to his wife, and he supports her in every way. Her name is Jules. And apparently Tanner raised Tucker's son, but I never learned the whole story."

"I have a great-grandson?" Ayita asked, her eyes glowing with joy.

"Two," Nikki replied. "Tanner and Jules have a two-year-old boy named Wyoming. Tucker's boy's name is Shawn. He's almost eighteen and very nice. You'd be proud of him, Grandmother. He has a good heart."

Ayita nodded. "Maybe someday I will know them all. What about the other?"

"Tucker? I never heard them speak of him."

"No. The one who holds your heart."

Nikki froze. She hadn't mentioned Mac or anyone else. How could Grandmother know? "There is no other," she managed to say.

Ayita nodded. "That's what you say, but it's what you don't speak that I hear."

Nikki couldn't answer. Would her grandmother not allow her to let the past go? It was the only way to ease the pain she felt. She *had* been wrong not to tell them from the beginning. But there was little she could do about it now, except try to forget and move on with her life. Someday it wouldn't hurt so much.

"Nioka?"

Swallowing the tears she knew would soon spill, Nikki answered. "He'll never forgive me for deceiving Tanner and Jules. Or him."

MAC LEANED ACROSS Shawn for a better view of Jules, who stood at the door of the white clapboard house that looked as old as the city of Tahlequah itself. Tanner sat quietly ahead of them in the driver's seat of the crew cab pickup.

"I remember this house," he said. "The yard is as neat and pretty as it was when I was a boy. I must have been five or six at the time."

"Sometimes the really good things never change," Mac replied, wishing he could turn back time. Not far, though. Two weeks would do it. Even one.

He'd spent the past week trying to come to terms with what had happened. Jules had told him several times that good people sometimes weren't able to be honest about something for a reason. It might not be right, but they were protecting themselves or someone else. Nikki had done that. After talking at length on the phone with his parents, Mac had realized they'd been protecting him. He understood now that Douglas MacGregor would always be his father, whether MacGregor blood ran in his veins or not.

Thinking of how much he'd learned over the past few days and hoping this visit would go well, he watched as Jules turned around, and he held his breath. She lifted her arm and… "Wait! Is Jules waving to us?"

"She is!" Shawn shouted, and was out the door and up the walk before anyone could answer.

"You go on, Tanner," Mac said. "I'll be along later."

Tanner reached for the handle and opened the door. "No. We all go together."

"But maybe family—"

"We're all family at the Rocking O. Remember?"

"Right."

As Tanner and Mac were getting out, Shawn returned. "She said to tell you that we need to park in the driveway of the house next door."

"Over there?" Mac asked, pointing to a row of tall bushes separating the two properties.

Shawn stepped closer. "Nikki's gone right now, and she's afraid that if Nikki sees the Suburban when she comes back, she'll leave."

Mac looked over the top of the vehicle at Tanner. "That's not a good sign."

Tanner nodded, his mouth turned down in a frown. "It's worse than I'd thought it would be. It's a good thing we brought Jules. She's much better at handling situations than I am."

"Better than me, too," Mac admitted.

Shawn walked around to the driver's side and slid onto the seat. "I'll move it."

Mac waited for Tanner, and they walked up the sidewalk together, joining Jules.

"Ayita," Jules said, "this is Tanner and our friend William MacGregor. You met Shawn. He's moving the car."

"Welcome," Ayita responded as they all walked past her and into the house. "My home is small, but I hope you can find someplace comfortable to sit. You've had a long drive."

"Thank you for seeing us," Tanner answered with a nervous smile. He waited until Ayita was sitting on an obviously well-loved easy chair, and then he sat on the end of the sofa closest to her. Jules sat next to him, and Mac chose the small sofa across from them.

Ayita smiled at Tanner. "You're an older version of

the little boy I remember. You've done well. Nioka says the ranch is beautiful."

"We're very proud of it. Somehow we've made it through the hard times."

"I watched your career over the many years. You have the talent of both your parents."

"I've retired from rodeo," he answered, taking his wife's hand. "Jules and I have a son. Wyoming will be two in October. I hope he'll get to meet you soon."

Ayita nodded and sighed. "I would like that very much."

When Shawn walked in the door, he hurried to sit next to Mac. "I don't think Nikki can see it if she comes from the west."

"She won't be looking for anyone," Ayita assured him, "but I thought it best not to let her know you are here. Mrs. O'Brien, there is lemonade in the kitchen. Would you mind getting everyone some?"

Jules glanced at Tanner with a smile before standing. "It's Jules, Ayita, and I'd be happy to. Shawn, would you come help me?"

"There are glasses in the cupboard and ice in the freezer," Ayita said as Jules and Shawn started for the kitchen. "If you hadn't told me who you are, Shawn, I would have thought you were Tucker."

Shawn ducked his head, obviously embarrassed. "That's what everyone says."

Tanner leaned forward. "Has he ever contacted you?"

Ayita shook her head, then looked up as the front door opened.

Mac's gaze followed Ayita's.

"Charlie said I could start on Monday," Nikki announced, tossing a set of keys to a nearby table and picking up a bundle of what appeared to be mail.

The heaviness Mac had felt in his chest eased, and his heart hammered. He'd come to terms with the reason for her deception, thanks to Jules and Kirby. She'd done the only thing she could do, considering how Tanner had felt about their mother. But Mac's joy at seeing her was dimmed by the fear that she would turn and leave when she realized they were all there.

"We've missed you, little sister," Tanner said, filling the silence in the room.

Nikki looked up, the envelopes falling from her hand. Her gaze darted around the room, finally lingering on Mac, and then on Tanner. "I…" She reached behind her for the door.

"Come sit by me, Nioka," Ayita said, her voice quiet yet firm. "Your family has come to see you."

Nikki hesitated, and then began to move, her steps unsteady as she walked to where her grandmother sat. Perching nervously on the arm of the chair, she glanced at her grandmother and took a deep breath before facing the others. "How did you find me?"

"Mac was convinced you'd come here," Tanner explained, "and I remembered where Ayita lived when I was a boy."

Nikki looked at Mac, then at Tanner. "But why are you all here?"

Jules stepped out of the kitchen, a glass in each hand. "Because we love you, Nikki, and we came to apologize."

Nikki shook her head. "You have nothing to apologize for. It's me who deceived everyone."

"Only because you thought you had to," Jules said softly as she walked into the room. She gave Ayita and

Tanner each a glass, then moved to place her hand on Nikki's shoulder. "You took us all by surprise, that's all. And we don't blame you for not telling us who you are. In the same situation I would do the same."

"Where's Kirby?" Nikki asked as Shawn walked in and handed a glass to Mac. "I tried to call Cheryl, but she's on vacation, and no one at OKDHS would tell me anything about him."

"He had an accident while with his father," Jules answered. "We'll talk about it later, but Kirby is back at the ranch and misses you."

Nikki jerked forward, fear written clearly on her face. "What happened?"

"A broken arm," Jules answered with a shrug, making it seem less than it was. "But we thought the long ride might be uncomfortable for him."

Seeing the sad smile on Nikki's face, Mac wished he could take her in his arms and assure her that all would be well, just as long as she came back to the ranch with them. "A lot has happened since you left."

When everyone started talking at once, Mac watched Ayita, her smile stretching wide and her eyes filling with tears. Would Nikki agree to return to the ranch, or would she choose this woman who had loved her since she was born?

"So you've heard nothing from Tucker?" Tanner was asking Ayita.

"He was here for a short while, two years or more after the man was here asking questions."

"That would have been the private detective I hired to find him."

"He was about the age of Shawn at the time," she answered, nodding. "He needed something only Charlie Brightwater could give him, so I sent him to Charlie at the school. He wasn't here for long, and he told me nothing about where he had been or where he was going."

"I wish I'd known," Tanner said, glancing at Jules.

"He asked me not to contact you," Ayita explained. "I argued, but it did no good, so I finally gave him my promise." She sighed. "So many promises have been made, and everyone is sadder because of them."

Tanner looked at Nikki, who now sat on the floor next to Ayita, her head in her grandmother's lap. "Not so much, now that Nikki has found us."

Nikki's smile was tentative, and she said nothing.

Feeling anxious, Mac decided it was time. Standing, he walked to where she was sitting and held out his hand. "Nikki, would you come outside with me?"

She leaned back, only a little, but the fear in her eyes said all he needed to know.

"Go on, Nioka," Ayita said. "The garden is blooming."

Nodding, Nikki took his hand and he helped her stand. "This way," she said, leading him toward the kitchen.

The garden was still beautiful, even in the last of autumn, as Nikki and Mac stepped out onto a flagstone patio at the back of the house. Instead of taking a seat on one of the many chairs filling the patio, Nikki remained standing and turned to look at him. "Why are we out here?" she asked.

"I know a simple apology isn't enough, but I don't know what else I can do."

"No," she answered with a small shake of her head. "I should be apologizing to everyone. What I did was unforgivable. I should have told Jules who I was when I applied for the job." Lowering her head, she sighed.

"My mother warned me that I wouldn't be accepted. She was right."

Lifting her chin with a finger, he forced her to look at him. "But you are. That's why we're here."

Her eyes glistened with tears and she turned away. "Maybe things are better as they are now."

"Bridey knew who you are."

She moved to look at him. "How?"

When he reached out and touched her cheek, she stood very still. "She recognized you when she first met you. You reminded her of her mother."

Nikki's eyes widened. "I did?" When he answered with a nod, she smiled.

"I have more to say, if you'll hear me out." When she nodded again, he moved closer. "I don't know how I can ever make up for what I did, but I'd like to take a lifetime to try."

Her eyes widened again and she took a step back. "I...I don't know what you mean."

He closed the space between them. "I love you, Nikki, with all my heart. I knew I shouldn't, and I tried not to, but every day I spent with you, I loved you a little more. I'm amazed by your kindness, the way you work with the boys and let them know how special they are to you. I've never met anyone like you, and I don't want to lose you."

Her gaze dropped. "I don't—"

"The boys need you. Kirby needs you." She seemed to waver, but said nothing. "And I need you."

She looked up, her teary gaze meeting his.

He was done wasting time. "I want you to be my wife."

"Oh, Mac, I—"

He pressed a finger to her lips. "If you're going to say no, please think again."

Behind him, he heard the sound of a door opening, then footsteps on the flagstone. Nikki looked up and he turned around.

Tanner walked toward them. "Don't say no, Nikki."

Jules followed, and they stopped next to Nikki. "And come back home with us."

"Please," Tanner added.

"I…" Nikki began, and then turned to look at Mac. "I've never even considered the possibility," she admitted. "But I can't deny that I love you, too, so I guess I'll have to accept."

Ignoring the others around them, who were laughing and cheering, he let out a yell and scooped her into her arms. "You won't be disappointed," he told her. "I'll spend my life making you happy."

"I'm already happy," she answered, pressing her palm to his cheek as tears filled her eyes. "There's nothing that could make me happier than to marry you."

"Don't be so sure of that."

"What do you mean?"

"It's all Jules's doing."

Nikki turned to her sister-in-law. "What is it?"

"Kirby won't be going back to his father," Jules explained. "I also managed to get Mac temporary guardianship, until all the necessary paperwork is done. Then Kirby can be adopted. Don't ask me how I did it," Jules said with a wave of her hand. "I can't tell you, but it's done."

"But adopted?" Nikki asked.

Mac smiled and held her closer. "By us, if that's what you want."

Her eyes danced with joy, and she kissed him, with

the whole family watching. "How can I ever thank you?" she whispered.

"Spending a lifetime with me," Mac answered. "But you might ask Jules and Tanner the same."

When she looked at Tanner, who stood with Jules and Shawn, he said, "You can come home with us. That's all the thanks we need. We're a family."

"A family," Nikki whispered. "I finally have a family."

Epilogue

Nikki wove her way through the friends and neighbors who had gathered at the ranch to share in her marriage to Mac. The early-spring day had dawned clear and cool, and she hadn't stopped smiling since it had begun.

But she didn't get far before Hettie Lambert stopped her. After a hug, Hettie stepped back. "I just want to know where you found your beautiful wedding dress, and then I'll leave you alone."

Nikki's smile widened. "Mac's mother had it made for me in Boston," she answered, smoothing her hand down the gleaming satin of her gown. "When she heard I wanted a traditional Cherokee wedding dress, she searched for someone who could make it."

"The beading is exquisite, and I love Mac's shirt."

"It's called a ribbon shirt," Nikki explained. "Another Cherokee custom."

Hettie leaned closer. "I'm so pleased to see Tanner accepting his Cherokee heritage."

"I am, too, but don't expect to see him wearing a headdress," Nikki added laughing.

Hettie turned to speak to someone else, and Tanner stepped up to Nikki. "Where did Sally go?" he asked, glancing around the yard. "I saw her during the ceremony, but haven't seen her since."

"She and Roger left shortly after the ceremony was over," Nikki replied, surprised that he'd recognized their mother.

"Why did she leave? I didn't even get to say hello to her."

Nikki could only tell him the truth. "She said this wasn't the time for the two of you to meet, after so many years, and thought it would be better to wait until another time."

Tanner nodded slowly, as if trying to grasp what it meant. "Maybe they can come for Shawn's graduation in May."

"I'm sure she'd love that," Nikki answered, smiling.

"There you are," a female voice rang out. Tanner moved away and Nikki turned to see Kate walking toward them, carrying one of her twin boys.

When Kate reached them, she sighed loudly. "Aunt Aggie needs you, Hettie. She's in the house with Bridey, and they can't seem to agree on whether gas or electric is best for cooking. I refuse to comment."

Hettie tipped her head back and laughed softly. "And they think I can settle it? I stopped cooking years ago. But I'll see what I can do."

When she was gone, Nikki turned to Kate. "I'm so glad you agreed to be a part of our wedding. I know your hands are full with the twins."

"We wouldn't have missed it for the world. We all wanted to be here." She looked at the eight-month-old she held and smiled. "Didn't we, Tyler? And Daddy has Travis, so we're all dandy."

Nikki looked up to see Trish and Paige walking toward them and waved. "All we need now is Jules."

"She's on her way," Kate answered with a nod of her head in the other direction. "In case you wondered, we planned to all be here together before you and Mac leave."

"You're all so wonderful," Nikki said as the others joined them.

"Kate, are you crying?" Paige asked.

Kate shook her head. "I never cry."

"Ha!" Trish said, adjusting the blanket on the baby girl in her arms. "Only when Dusty proposed, her wedding, my wedding, when I went into labor with Krista—"

"Okay, okay," Kate admitted. "There are those moments. Like this one."

Nikki felt tears of her own, thinking of the joy they all shared.

Paige brought her back to earth. "I'm supposed to remind you that it's time to leave, Nikki, so we'd better wrap this up."

Each of Nikki's friends produced a new silver dollar, while Paige explained. "It's a tradition in my family for the bride's closest friends to give her a shiny new coin on her wedding day for luck."

Nikki looked through misty eyes at the silver in her hand, and knew she was blessed.

"Time for you to be off on the adventure of your new life," Trish said, her voice thick with emotion.

When they'd dried their tears, they joined the rest of the wedding party and guests. Nikki wiped the last of her tears with the back of her hand and smiled. This was what she had always dreamed of, being part of a big, caring family. And now she had it. All of it.

Tanner, standing beside her, pulled her into a hug. "We're going to miss you, little sister."

Nikki smiled and looked up at him, the threat of more tears stinging her eyes. "I'm going to miss you, too. All of you. But we won't be gone so long. We'll be back before Shawn graduates."

When Tanner released her, Mac, holding Kirby's hand, slipped an arm around her waist and pulled her close. "I won't have her to myself for long. She has a long list of EAP seminars to attend for accreditation. Somehow, though, we'll squeeze in a *little* honeymooning."

But Nikki wasn't listening to what Mac was saying. Across the new spring green of the lawn of the Rocking O, she could see a man coming toward them. He walked with a limp and leaned on a cane, but his approach was determined.

As he drew nearer, Nikki recognized him. He'd been to the school when she was twelve, and he'd been a student there for a few weeks. He'd also visited her grandmother, but she hadn't made a connection. Now she did.

Slipping away from Mac, she walked toward their visitor.

"Where are you going?" Mac called to her.

She didn't answer. Mac would understand when he knew. And so would the others.

When she reached the man, he gave her a wry smile. "You grew up, Nikki," he said.

"So did you, Tucker."

* * * * *

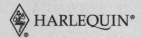
HARLEQUIN®

American ★ Romance®

COMING NEXT MONTH

Available November 9, 2010

#1329 THE SHERIFF'S CHRISTMAS SURPRISE
Babies & Bachelors USA
Marie Ferrarella

#1330 JESSE: MERRY CHRISTMAS, COWBOY
The Codys: The First Family of Rodeo
Lynnette Kent

#1331 SANTA IN A STETSON
Fatherhood
Rebecca Winters

#1332 MIRACLE BABY
Baby To Be
Laura Bradford

REQUEST YOUR FREE BOOKS!
2 FREE NOVELS PLUS 2 FREE GIFTS!

HARLEQUIN®

American Romance®

Love, Home & Happiness!

YES! Please send me 2 FREE Harlequin® American Romance® novels and my 2 FREE gifts (gifts are worth about $10). After receiving them, if I don't wish to receive any more books, I can return the shipping statement marked "cancel." If I don't cancel, I will receive 4 brand-new novels every month and be billed just $4.24 per book in the U.S. or $4.99 per book in Canada. That's a saving of at least 15% off the cover price! It's quite a bargain! Shipping and handling is just 50¢ per book.* I understand that accepting the 2 free books and gifts places me under no obligation to buy anything. I can always return a shipment and cancel at any time. Even if I never buy another book from Harlequin, the two free books and gifts are mine to keep forever.

154/354 HDN E5LG

Name _____ (PLEASE PRINT)

Address _____ Apt. #

City _____ State/Prov. _____ Zip/Postal Code

Signature (if under 18, a parent or guardian must sign)

Mail to the **Harlequin Reader Service:**
IN U.S.A.: P.O. Box 1867, Buffalo, NY 14240-1867
IN CANADA: P.O. Box 609, Fort Erie, Ontario L2A 5X3

Not valid for current subscribers to Harlequin® American Romance® books.

Want to try two free books from another line?
Call 1-800-873-8635 or visit www.morefreebooks.com.

* Terms and prices subject to change without notice. Prices do not include applicable taxes. N.Y. residents add applicable sales tax. Canadian residents will be charged applicable provincial taxes and GST. Offer not valid in Quebec. This offer is limited to one order per household. All orders subject to approval. Credit or debit balances in a customer's account(s) may be offset by any other outstanding balance owed by or to the customer. Please allow 4 to 6 weeks for delivery. Offer available while quantities last.

Your Privacy: Harlequin is committed to protecting your privacy. Our Privacy Policy is available online at www.eHarlequin.com or upon request from the Reader Service. From time to time we make our lists of customers available to reputable third parties who may have a product or service of interest to you. If you would prefer we not share your name and address, please check here. ☐

Help us get it right—We strive for accurate, respectful and relevant communications. To clarify or modify your communication preferences, visit us at www.ReaderService.com/consumerschoice.

HARI0R

*See below for a sneak peek from
our inspirational line, Love Inspired® Suspense*

*Enjoy this heart-stopping excerpt from
RUNNING BLIND
by top author Shirlee McCoy,
available November 2010!*

**The mission trip to Mexico was supposed to be an
adventure. But the thrill turns sour when Jenna Dougherty
and her roommate Magdalena are kidnapped.**

"It's okay. I'm here to help." The voice was as deep as the
darkness, but Jenna Dougherty didn't believe the lie. She
could do nothing but lie still as hands slid down her arms,
felt the rope around her wrists.

"I'm going to use a knife to cut you free, Jenna. Hold
still."

The cold blade of a knife pressed close to her head before
her gag fell away.

"I—" she started, but her mouth was dry, and she could
do nothing but suck in air.

"Shhh. Whatever needs to be said can be said when
we're out of here." Nick spoke quietly, his hand gentle on
her cheek. There and gone as he sliced through the ropes on
her wrists and ankles.

He pulled her upright. "Come on. We may be on
borrowed time."

"I can't leave my friend," Jenna rasped out.

"There's no one here. Just us."

"She has to be here." Jenna took a step away.

"There's no one here. Let's go before that changes."

"It's dark. Maybe if we find a light…"

"What did you say?"

"We need to turn on the light. I can't leave until I know that—"

"What can you see, Jenna?"

"Nothing."

"No shadows? No light?"

"No."

"It's broad daylight. There's light spilling in from the window I climbed in through. You can't see it?"

She went cold at his words.

"I can't see anything."

"You've got a nasty bruise on your forehead. Maybe that has something to do with it." His fingers traced the tender flesh on her forehead.

"It doesn't matter *how* it happened. I'm blind!"

Can Nick help Jenna find her friend or will chasing this trail have Jenna running blindly again into danger?

Find out in RUNNING BLIND, available in November 2010 only from Love Inspired Suspense.